EVIDENTIALLY GUILTY

Jeffrey Ashford titles available from
Severn House Large Print

Fair Exchange is Robbery
Looking-Glass Justice
A Truthful Injustice

EVIDENTIALLY GUILTY

Jeffrey Ashford

Severn House Large Print
London & New York

This first large print edition published in Great Britain 2005 by
SEVERN HOUSE LARGE PRINT BOOKS LTD of
9-15 High Street, Sutton, Surrey, SM1 1DF.
First world regular print edition published 2004 by
Severn House Publishers, London and New York.
This first large print edition published in the USA 2005 by
SEVERN HOUSE PUBLISHERS INC., of
595 Madison Avenue, New York, NY 10022.

British Library Cataloguing in Publication Data

Ashford, Jeffrey, 1926 -
    Evidentially guilty - Large print ed.
    1.   Harassment - Fiction
    2.   Detective and mystery stories
    3.   Large type books
    I.   Title
    823.9'14 [F]

    ISBN 0-7278-7415-2

Printed and bound in Great Britain by
MPG Books Ltd, Bodmin, Cornwall.

One

Jerome Dean turned off the road on to the tarmacked area at the side of the head keeper's cottage and braked to a halt alongside a Bentley Continental. He crossed to where Russell was talking to a man who wore the loudest check suit he'd seen on the shooting field – or off it, come to that.

'Morning, Jerome,' Russell boomed, his voice deep and cheerful, matching his figure. 'Got your eye well in, I hope! Jeanes says they'll be flying high if the wind stays.'

'In other words, too high for us?'

Russell smiled. 'You don't expect him to allow we're up to his birds ... Jerome, I'd like you to meet Louis – Baron Vaillant.'

'It is a pleasure to meet,' Vaillant said, his words strongly accented, as they shook hands. It seemed clear the meeting afforded him little pleasure.

'Jerome is our Annie Oakley,' Russell observed.

'I do not understand.'

'The heroine of the musical *Annie Get Your Gun*.'

'I do not enjoy American musicals.'

'Then you're missing a lot. Which is more than she did.'

'How is that?'

'Annie was a crack marksman – markswoman, in these times of equality? – who used to shoot cigarettes from her husband's lips.'

'I prefer to be married to a woman who does not shoot cigarettes from my lips.'

'In case she decides to be off aim for once?'

Vaillant was not amused.

'There's Tig, as usual arriving at the last moment. Excuse me while I have a word with him.' Russell, his shooting suit appearing even more ancient and worn in contrast to Vaillant's, crossed to a BMW that had drawn into the parking area.

'Are you here on holiday?' Dean asked.

'I am here for work.' A loyal Frenchman, he would not have visited England by choice.

6

'There seem to be quite a few of your countrymen working here these days; in fact, I've met a couple recently, both in the financial markets.'

'Indeed,' Vaillant said dismissively.

In the interests of social entente cordiale, Dean tried to keep the conversation alive. 'Is this the first time you've shot at Ister?'

'Yes.'

'Then you're in for a treat. The birds are always well presented; but if there's a wind from the west, as there is today, some of them will be up in the stratosphere. They can be very damaging to one's ego.'

'Not if one shoots well.'

A tall, thin man, with a beaky face, walked up to them. 'Morning, Jerome. Where's Kay?'

'Leo's going to a party this afternoon and that always threatens to raise his excitement to fever pitch, so she decided to stay at home and keep him as calm as possible ... May I introduce you to...' Dean stopped as Vaillant walked away.

Marks stared at the departing figure. 'The last time I saw a suit like that, it was at the circus. Is he a Frenchman?'

'Baron Louis Vaillant.'

'Extraordinary how a country providing *haute couture* to women, can only offer *basse couture* to men.'

Jeanes, solidly built, his face moulded by sun, wind and rain, an old Barbour jacket and leggings over a keeper's suit, walked up to where Russell stood. 'All ready, sir.'

'Right. I'll pick the stands and then we'll take off.' He looked up at the nearest oak tree, whose leaves, still only lightly touched by a late autumn, were moving to the wind. 'They should be tall birds at Bourne Wood.'

'I reckon.'

'You'll take the beat really slowly?'

'Wasn't reckoning on doing it at the gallop.' Jeanes was annoyed at the suggestion he might not control the beating expertly. He crossed to a Land Rover, settled behind the wheel, and drove off.

Russell brought from the pocket of his jacket a leather case inside which were eight ivory pegs in a wooden holder. He held the holder out to the nearest man, who withdrew one of the pegs. 'Eight.'

'Longstop for the curlers at the first beat; they'll keep you guessing,' Russell said, before he moved on to offer the draw to the other six guns.

Dean withdrew the seventh peg. 'Two.'

'Good. That puts you in the pound seats at Bourne.' Russell took back the peg, replaced it with the others in the holder, closed the case. 'Let's get moving, then,' he called out.

Land Rovers carried the eight guns, wives, female companions, two loaders – despite the fact it was not double guns – and dogs, to the first beat. Stands were marked with numbered pegs and Dean walked up the broad ride to number 2, at the right-angle corner of one of the smaller woods. The first rule in the field: know where the other guns are. He checked to his right: Brennigan, his wife by his side, his loader behind him. By the wife was a tethered cocker spaniel. The dog had been trained at great expense and was a field trial champion, but Brennigan never tried to work it himself and seldom showed any interest in or affection for it – a trained dog was as necessary to the image of a sportsman as a pair of Holland and Hollands. His wife was known, behind her back, as The Battleaxe.

Dean looked to his left. Vaillant, in his unmistakable suit, which would surely amuse any pheasant, was repeatedly raising his gun to his shoulder and sweeping it through an arc, his action looking less smooth than he probably thought.

Dean broke his gun, loaded, closed it and checked the safety catch was on – an unnecessary action, since the closing automatically set it, but one could never be too careful where guns were concerned. He ran his right hand along the top of the cartridges in his belt, confirming it was filled; he looked down at his bag on the ground to make certain it was open and more cartridges immediately available.

There was a distant shout, which would have aroused Jeanes's wrath since he demanded sharp discipline from the beaters, despite the resentment this caused among the younger ones. 'If you don't like it, you can bugger off,' was his invariable reply to any complaint. Very few did so. They liked the open-air exercise, the sport, the possibility of seeing well-known names in the flesh, the two bottles of rum at lunch time, the crisp fivers at the end of the day.

A pigeon, with dipping flight, came into view above the trees ahead of Dean. He raised his gun, slipping forward the safety catch with the thumb of his right hand. As his finger curled around the for'd trigger, there was a shot, followed by another; the pigeon jinked to its right and made its escape. Dean lowered his gun, engaging the safety catch as he did so. Since the pigeon had been coming straight over him, it had been his bird and Vaillant had been poaching.

There was a flush of pheasants on the right, a barrage of shots, a pause. Some thirty yards into the woods ahead of Dean was a low flushing fence and he watched several birds running along it; suddenly, one rose and was immediately followed by four more. He gained a good right and left, the second bird dropping well back; he heard a picker-up's whistle guide his dog on the retrieve.

Three birds broke over Vaillant; he fired both barrels and missed. A solitary cock, tail streaming, which had flushed well back, came directly towards Dean at speed. As he raised his gun, Vaillant fired both barrels and missed. Dean pulled the for'd trigger and the cock's head jerked up, its body arched, and it crashed to the ground well behind. Another attempted poach. Vaillant was either ignorant of, or indifferent to, the etiquette in a shooting field.

The tapping of the beaters' sticks became audible. A fox appeared and disappeared. Foxes always raised the problem: to shoot, or not to shoot – that was the question. Whether to please the keeper or raise the ire of any gun a keen huntsman ...?

There was a last flush of birds, all of which Dean let pass because, for some inexplicable reason, they were low. He noted, without surprise, that Vaillant continued to lack any judgement – all that flew was grist to his gun. The beaters broke cover and stood around until curt orders from Jeanes sent them forward to the next beat. As Dean finished collecting his birds, a picker-up added five to those already by his peg, saying they were his and had fallen behind in the wood; the G.S.P., shortened tail wagging, was restlessly eager to return to work and had to be verbally restrained.

His gun broken and across his left forearm, Dean walked along the line. As he neared the next peg, at which there were only three pheasants, Vaillant said aggressively, 'You have some of my birds.'

'I'm sorry if I've made a mistake,' he said, knowing he hadn't.

'Please do not do it again.'

He walked on, amused that the Frenchman should so resent an obvious lack of success.

West, tall, thin, with a face hewn rather than formed, joined him as he neared the waiting Land Rovers and asked how he'd got on. With typical modesty, he replied he'd missed some birds he should have brought down. West laughed. 'You miss one, Jerome, it's supercharged!'

He climbed into the back of the first vehicle and had to squeeze up against The Battleaxe. She asked how Kay was, did not bother to listen to his answer, told him – and everyone else within earshot – that the government's taxation policies were reducing her to penniless starvation. A little light starvation would have benefited her figure; the jewellery she wore would have kept many people fed generously for a long time.

The Land Rover stopped and they climbed out on to the wide ride that separated two halves of a large wood. As they disembarked, The Battleaxe – after demanding the help of two men to enable her to climb down to the ground – gave her opinion of the local council.

A gun moved two numbers at each stand,

making certain he would enjoy one of the favoured central positions, over which most birds could be expected to fly, at least once during the day. Dean walked along the uneven grassland, still damp from the previous night's rain, to peg number 4. He dropped the cartridge bag, flap open, confirmed the belt was full and, after loading, checked the safety catch. This beat should produce birds almost as good as at Bourne Wood; the land in front sloped upwards and the trees – ancient oaks – would force them high.

He held the gun slackly, ready to bring it up in one smooth motion that would bed the butt firmly into his shoulder, the muzzle beginning its sweep. He was a modest man, yet accepted to himself that he was a good, perhaps even first-class, shot; he enjoyed the art of being able to gauge height, speed, direction, and aim-off, with pinpoint accuracy, which was why he was frequently asked to Ister – that and the fact that Kay was a cousin of George Russell.

Two pigeons came over and, having been flushed way back, were very high. Dean did not fire, judging them to be out of shot; Vaillant loosed off both barrels. He shouted at the nearest picker-up to watch both birds because they were hard hit.

Missed by yards, Dean judged. He was surprised Vaillant had been asked to the shoot, since he was not only a poor marksman, he had no idea how to behave. Yet Russell, who had served in the Navy before his elder brother had died suddenly and the estate had become his, usually ran a very 'tiddly-tight' ship.

A relatively low hen pheasant flew over Vaillant, was greeted with both barrels and flew on, unscathed. Two high, fast cocks came over Dean and were downed.

A rabbit running from right to left, desperately zig zagging, as if danger lay behind, not to its side, passed number 3 gun, who, observing the unwritten rules, did not shoot since the beaters were approaching; Dean watched it for a brief moment, then once more stared up. From Dean's left came a single shot. There was a high-pitched scream. He saw a man, hands on his stomach, rise up out of a large patch of brambles some fifteen feet into the woods and, as he watched, momentarily too shocked to do anything, the man collapsed.

Two

'Terrible, terrible,' Russell said for the umpteenth time as he stood by the side of the cottage.

'What the hell was he doing there?' Marks said, for the umpteenth time.

'God knows!'

'He wasn't one of the beaters who'd got lost?'

'Jeanes has never seen him before, nor has any of the other beaters.'

'I must say, he didn't look too good when they put him into the ambulance.'

'The paramedic reckoned it was likely to be touch and go ... Goddamnit! I've always tried to run the shoot safely, but this makes nonsense of that.'

'I don't see you can hold yourself in any way responsible.'

Russell produced a cigarette case and, as

he opened and offered it, his hand was shaking.

'Who shot him?' Marks asked, as he took a cigarette. 'With the lie of the land, presumably it could only be Jerome, Bill, or that Frenchman?'

'Wouldn't like to give an opinion.' Russell spoke uneasily. He flicked open a lighter and, the flame jiggling as his hand continued to shake, held it out.

'To shoot low with the beaters approaching, it had to be a bloody fool. So it couldn't have been Jerome or Bill, could it?'

'How the hell am I supposed to know?'

'Sorry.'

Russell drew on the cigarette, exhaled. 'I keep asking myself, can I be to blame?'

'Look, George, stop thinking like that. As I've said, there's no way you could know some fool had come into the woods on a shooting day or that an even bigger fool was going to shoot low.'

'Maybe not. Only it's my shoot, I organize things...'

'You're no more at fault than someone lending a car to a friend who gets drunk and mows down a pedestrian.'

'Depends if you know he's a hard drinker.'

'Did you know the Frenchman was a careless gun?'

'Don't know a damn thing about him. I was asked as a favour to invite him to the shoot by an old friend.'

'Wasn't doing you any favours.'

'For some reason the powers that be in London want him in a good humour and thought this might help.' Russell dropped the cigarette and ground it out with his heel. 'When are they going to start moving?' he muttered, as he stared once more at the PC.

'It's bound to take time.'

Russell looked at his watch. 'Jeanes says his wife wants to know what to do about lunch – should she go ahead and finish the cooking?'

'If you're open to suggestions, tell her to go ahead. The police will probably have to talk to each of us and all the beaters before they let anyone go, so a meal would come in handy.'

'You could be right.'

'And a drink wouldn't go amiss; help to steady nerves.'

The PC was a morose man – doubly so, since his free weekend had been interrupted. He took preliminary statements in the sitting room of Jeanes's cottage, seated on one side of the small table brought through from the kitchen. 'Can I have your name, sir?' By choice, he did not call anyone 'sir', but the people he was having to deal with expected respect – though God knew why – and would become more helpful if granted it.

'Jerome Dean.'

'Your address?'

'Kingslee Farm. That's a small village...'

'I know where it is.' No ardent socialist, he still knew moments when he was aggrieved that there were those able to lead a far more comfortable life than he. 'You were the nearest to where the victim was shot?'

'Number four peg.'

'I'm not certain what that means.'

'I'm no artist, but will it help if I sketch a plan?'

'I reckon.'

'Do you have something to draw on?'

The PC hesitated, then pushed across his opened notebook and a ballpoint pen.

Dean drew the main ride, the cross ride, the corner of the wood, and the positions of the eight guns. He passed the notebook back. The PC made a brief note of the circumstances in which the sketch had been made before he looked up. 'As you've said, you were at number four when the victim was shot?'

'That's right.'

'So what happened?'

'There was a single shot to my left and almost immediately a man screamed. I looked into the woods and saw a man, in the middle of a clump of brambles, who was clutching his stomach. He collapsed. I ran forward. It was obvious he was seriously injured, so I called out to ask if anyone had a mobile; one of the guns did and he called an ambulance.'

'Do you know who fired the shot that hit the victim?'

'All I can really say is, it was not I.'

'Is there anything more you can tell me?'

'I don't think there is.'

'That's all, then, and you can leave. You understand someone will be along to take a fuller statement from you?'

'Of course.'

'Thank you for your help, sir.' The PC was annoyed he'd said that. Where was the point in thanking a man for doing what he was obliged to do? Especially when the other's apparent helpful manner possibly concealed a patronizing contempt for PC Plod.

Kingslee Farm was a typical sixteenth-century, timber framed house with peg tiles and a long, sharp-sloping, south-facing roof providing an outshut. Despite proof to the contrary, local tradition maintained that Marshall, one of the leaders of the nineteenth-century smuggling gang that had terrorized the neighbourhood over several years, had lived there. Dean would always have described himself as reasonably practical and down-to-earth, but in this instance he preferred fiction to fact, since it allowed him to imagine the motley gang wending their way to the darkened house, ponies laden with brandy, baccy, laces and letters.

He drove into the garage – a barn of no great age or consequence – and from the boot of the silver estate lifted out leather leg-of-mutton gun case, cartridge bag, and four unopened boxes of cartridges. He walked down the gravel path to the garden gate, then along the brick path to the small porch, a modern addition. As he stepped into the hall – where animals had once been kept; perhaps where the ponies had been relieved of their loads – Kay came out of the sitting room, the top of her hair only just clearing the header. 'You're back early – didn't expect you before five as it was the main coverts. Nothing wrong, I hope?'

'Nothing that affects me,' he answered quickly, knowing that with any hesitation on his part, she would envisage a dozen calamities. A strong-willed woman, yet if anything threatened him or Leo, she panicked.

'You sound as if something has happened?'

'A man got shot.'

'My God! One of the guns or a beater?'

'An unknown.'

'What's that mean?'

'We were on the second beat, there was a shot, and a man appeared from the middle of a large clump of brambles and collapsed. When I got to him, he was only semi-conscious and bleeding from the stomach. No one had any idea who he was. The police will be trying to identify him now.'

'The police?'

'George called them to report what had happened since it was a shooting accident. They took statements from all of us.'

'But why, if it was an accident?'

'I imagine fatal accidents are always investigated fairly thoroughly, probably to see if safety regulations have been observed; and in this case, there's the need to identify him and get in touch with relatives. And for my money, there's the added fact that the accident was the result of stupid carelessness even though there was no way of knowing someone was in the brambles.'

'Why was it so careless?'

'You know the second stand in Tarka's Wood?'

She thought for a moment. 'Yes.'

'The land slopes upwards and the undergrowth is pretty dense so one can't see any distance. With the beaters approaching, only an incompetent is going to fire low.'

'Do you know who it was?'

'The chap on my left, a Frenchman who'd already shown himself incompetent – didn't seem to have any idea how to behave in the field. God knows why George ever invited him.'

'He must be terribly shocked?'

'George, yes; Vaillant, probably not, from the way he was behaving.'

'But you're certain it was he?'

'The shot came from my left, Tig and Bill were round the corner of the wood and almost certainly the lie of the land made it impossible for them to have hit the man. In any case, have you ever seen either of them firing low into overgrown ground with the beaters advancing?'

'Do the police know all this?'

'I've no idea.'

'Then you didn't tell them?'

'I just said a single shot was fired to my left immediately before the man appeared out of the brambles.'

'Why didn't you explain it had to be this Frenchman?'

'Because ... I know it's going to sound damned silly, but I didn't want to lay the blame.'

'No sneaking?'

'I said, damned silly.'

She moved forward, lightly gripped his right arm. 'Just typical. And thank God for that! ... I imagine you're starving?' She released his arm.

'We ate there. Jeanes's wife had prepared the meal and the questioning was obviously going to take time, so George decided it seemed reasonable, despite what had happened.'

'Always the practical man.'

'Ironically, he hardly ate anything because he was in such a state of nerves. Blaming himself, despite the fact he'd absolutely no reason to do so.'

'I don't suppose you ate much.'

'Couldn't get over the shock of hearing the man scream and collapse; seeing the blood.'

'Then I'll get you something now.'

'I'm not certain...'

'I am. And you'll have a stiff drink while you're waiting ... Damn! I promised to help Jane when it's feeding time at the zoo. Oh well, she'll just have to suffer on her own the consequences of holding a party for five- and six-year-olds.'

Three

Only Curran and Tudor were in the CID general room. 'I can never understand the pleasure of shooting birds,' Curran remarked.

'That's because you're not a gentleman.'

'If the birds could shoot back, they'd soon pack it in, gentlemen or peasants.'

'If your roast beef could talk, you'd become a vegetarian.'

'What I eat is killed to keep me alive.'

'Equally reprehensible.'

'Remind me to laugh.'

The phone, attached to a long lead, had been left on the fifth desk; it rang. Curran was closer to it, but Tudor was not surprised when the other made no move. He stood, threaded his way between the desks, lifted the receiver. 'CID, Redford.'

'The shot man has been identified as

26

Keith Hopkins. Address: Two, Well Road.'

'Is that in this town, sir?'

'I'd have said if it wasn't. The occupant is to be informed that Hopkins is at Ranleigh General, in intensive care. Find out what he was doing on the land.' The connexion was cut.

Tudor replaced the receiver, returned to his desk. Had Naylor ever considered giving an order pleasantly, rather than in parade-ground style? Probably not. The detective inspector had all the grace of a two-headed cobra. 'The guv'nor says the shot man is Keith Hopkins and someone's to go along to his place in Well Road, tell his missus what's happened, and find out what he was doing there.'

'Then what keeps you standing about?'

'It's your turn. I went to Allerton earlier.'

'Becoming bolshie, are we?'

Guilty of careless optimism. Curran would never willingly do anything except leave for home. 'Do you know where Well Road is?'

'How about the other side of the hospital?' Curran sniggered.

'Give me a break. I don't want to spend all afternoon and evening looking for it.'

'You know the Rose and Crown, near the

station? It's two or three roads behind there.' Curran leaned back in his chair. 'You wouldn't think it now, but it was once a smart area. Several of the forty thieves had houses there before the neighbourhood went downhill.'

'Forty thieves?'

'Local businessmen who had their fingers into everything, including other people's tills ... Come to think of it, it was just off Well Road I collared the fingerman everyone had been after for weeks. The rest chased after where he'd been; I used history to work out where he'd likely do his next job and was waiting for him.'

In his own mind, Tudor thought, Curran outsmarted everyone. Which raised the question: how did he explain his lack of promotion? 'I'll get moving.'

'Watch the snails don't get there first.'

Tudor left, passed the detective sergeant's and detective inspector's rooms, arrived at the lift to find it was still out of order. Canteen buzz said the maintenance firm was refusing to make the repairs until their last bill was paid. For once, rumour might be correct. C division was short of money, as was every other division. The government had promised the necessary funding to promote the improved policing needed, but that promise had proved to be just one more political Fata Morgana.

The CID Ford Escort had been parked in the inspector's bay; this would result in an ill-tempered note to Naylor and that, in turn, would result in a bollocking for the guilty DC. 'It's not the criminals get right up my nose,' a PC had recently remarked, 'it's senior officers who expect to be treated like they walk on water.'

The Escort was reluctant to start. Servicing had been delayed to spread the cost, even though that had become a matter of internal accounting since Vehicles now serviced the force's cars (after they'd serviced their own, of course). Finally, the engine fired. He backed, turned, drove up to the exit and waited for passing traffic, then drew out behind a white Transit van, which was heavily laden. On the smuggling run? Buying tobacco and alcohol in Belgium or France and selling it cheaper than it would cost in England, but still at a considerable profit? Because the motorways were being patrolled more actively by the speed coppers, following a governmental demand for a crackdown on the booze run, the smarter drivers were keeping off them and using A roads.

He stopped at traffic lights. The building on the far side was being demolished and a large noticeboard announced it was to be replaced by one more chain store. Fifty years before, Redford had been a quiet market town, possessing the quirky charms of having grown haphazardly over the centuries; now, it was little different from a hundred and one other towns where chain store followed chain store and small, independent shops, offering quality, had vanished.

He watched a brunette walk along the pavement. She didn't resemble Hazel, yet to see her was to think of Hazel. Which he did, until a car behind hooted and brought his mind back to the present and the green light. He drove on. Would there be a Hazel at number 2, wondering where her man had got to? He hoped he'd have to speak to a man, not a woman, because men usually accepted bad news without overt emotion. The worst job of a policeman was to have to impart bad news to a wife and watch her struggle not to accept that she was being dragged down into a whirlpool of tragedy and need.

As he turned into Well Road, he doubted this had ever been a smart area, as Curran had claimed. The semi-detached houses lacked any architectural character and the front gardens were too mean to provide more than a hint of colour. He parked, crossed the pavement to number 2, opened the wrought-iron gate, which squealed, walked up the narrow path of imitation York stone, stepped into the shallow porch and rang the front-door bell. From inside came a few bars from 'Home, Sweet Home'. Appropriately naff!

The door was opened by a man whom Tudor automatically docketed. Early thirties, slightly built and no athlete; tight curly black hair topped a face that, confusingly, suggested both weakness and determination; mouth was slightly crooked; clothes were casual, but possessed a smartness not normally seen in areas like Well Road. 'My name's Detective Constable Tudor, local CID.'

Apprehension was immediate.

'May I come in?' Tudor stepped into the hall, on the walls of which hung four paintings, each a formless explosion of colour.

'Would you tell me what your name is?'

There was no answer.

'May I have your name, please?'

'Something's wrong,' he said wildly, hissing the "s" so that it sounded like "sh". 'Something's happened to Keith. It has, hasn't it?'

'You are a friend of Mr Hopkins?'

'We live here.'

'Your name is ...?'

'Edgar.'

'Edgar what?'

'Lynch.'

'I'm sorry to have to tell you, Mr Lynch, that Mr Hopkins has been involved in a shooting accident.'

Lynch stared at Tudor for several seconds before he said, in mumbling tones: 'Is he ... Is he badly hurt?'

'All I can tell you is that, at the moment, he is in intensive care at Ranleigh General Hospital.'

'He's dying!'

Even though bitter experience had taught him the futility, even hypocrisy, of this, Tudor tried to offer reason for comfort. 'He may be under constant observation just to make certain he's doing reasonably well.'

Lynch began to sob; his thin shoulders shook.

Tudor remembered his earlier hope that he would have to give the bad news to a man, not a woman, because then his own emotional stress would be less. Ironic, since now he was facing a man who was incapable of suppressing his overwhelming grief. He spoke with authority; authority deleted choice. 'I'm sorry, but I have to ask you one or two questions.'

'Which hospital is he in? I must go there in case he ... in case...'

'The staff will be doing everything possible. And I promise to be as brief as I can, so shall we go into a room and sit?'

Lynch, his expression one of shocked bewilderment, opened the door to his right and went into the front room, decorated and furnished in colours almost as chaotic as those in the pictures in the hall. He crossed to the window and stared out at the road.

'Mr Hopkins was in a wood on the Ister estate when there was a shoot in progress. Would you know why he was there?'

'I told him not to.' Lynch turned suddenly, brought his right fist down on the arm of the settee, the force of the blow causing a tear to fall from his cheek. 'Don't go, I said, I can feel something terrible will happen if you do. He laughed. He always laughs when I say I can tell what's going to happen; he'll tell me to know something useful, like what's going to win the Derby. I begged him, if not for his sake, for mine. But he said he had to go and stop the murdering bastards. It was his duty as a decent human being.'

'Who was he trying to stop?' Tudor asked, wondering if grief was unhinging the other's mind.

'The people shooting birds in the name of sport.'

'Mr Hopkins was an animal-rights activist?'

Lynch nodded, covered his face with his hands.

Four

Detective Inspector Naylor, shorter than he would have wished since height could command respect, stouter than was medically advisable because his wife was a good cook, sat behind a desk on which, in a neat pile, were numerous memoranda from County HQ. Had he been of a more independent character, he would have thrown them all into the waste-paper basket. 'Did Lynch say if Hopkins was a member of any known organization?'

'I asked, sir, but received a meaningless answer,' Tudor said. 'He was in a hell of an emotional state.'

'What could Hopkins have thought he was going to do?'

'I had a word with one of the lads who does some beating in his off-duty hours – beating the woods, that is.'

'It is not part of your job to try to be humorous.'

'No, sir.' He wondered why he had tried to make a feeble joke: Naylor had no sense of humour. 'He says the pheasants have to be moved forward slowly and skilfully because if they panic and flush, they go over the guns in a rush, instead of in ones and twos. His best guess is that Hopkins intended to appear suddenly, panicking the oncoming birds and forcing them on to the wing in all directions, ruining the beat.'

'You're saying he was hiding in the brambles, intending to pop up like a jack-in-the-box?'

'I'm not, sir; Steve is.'

Naylor rubbed his square, cleft chin with fingers that were surprisingly slender for a man of bulk. 'Sounds daft.'

'Some of these animal activists seem to thrive on daft ideas.'

The phone rang. Naylor answered the call. Tudor shifted his weight from one foot to the other. The DI might have suggested he sat; it wouldn't have diminished his authority. A great man for maintaining an air of authority. Because he knew it was his rank, not he, that provided it? According to Jigger,

Naylor had only been made DI because there had been a vacancy that had had to be quickly filled after a DI, arguing with his DCI, had suddenly keeled over, dead; but for that stroke of luck, Naylor would have remained a detective sergeant, better at obeying orders than giving them and perhaps happier doing so.

Naylor replaced the phone. 'Hopkins died half an hour ago. They did their best, but too many organs had been damaged. At what range was he shot?'

'I couldn't say.'

'Didn't you map the scene?'

'PC Fleet attended the incident, sir, not me.'

'And you haven't spoken to him to ascertain the relevant details?'

And hadn't done a hundred and one other things that hindsight suggested he might have done, but foresight hadn't.

'Make certain of the distances.' He began to drum on the desk with the fingers of his right hand. 'This death complicates things.'

Certainly for Hopkins and Lynch, Tudor thought. And for himself, come to that. It was nearly six thirty on a Saturday night and he was supposed to be taking Hazel to a disco, having returned home, bathed and eaten.

'There may have been criminal negligence and we'll have to consider manslaughter ... Has the person who fired the fatal shot been identified?'

'Not as far as I know.'

'You have a list of the people who were shooting?'

'PC Fleet probably has that.'

'You seem to be certain of very little.'

'Not my case, sir.'

'I've said before, our work cannot be compartmentalized.'

Quite. Whatever that meant.

'Tell Sergeant Unwin I want each gun questioned, and anyone else who can help, to determine who was responsible for Hopkins's death. And I want that started right away.' The rate at which his fingers tapped increased. 'It could be tricky since they won't be the usual run of suspects; likely some of them will be ... We'll need to take things very carefully. Make it clear that the questioning must be discreetly carried out.'

'Let our own discretion be our tutor?'

'What's that?'

'Nothing, sir.'

'I've no time for someone who tries to be smart.'

There was a silence, which Naylor broke. 'You've already forgotten I said I want inquiries to be started right away, not next week?'

Tudor left and went into the next room; the detective sergeant was not there. Unwin, like many an old hand, had the knack of not being around when work beckoned. With any luck, he thought, Steve Fleet would also be no one knew where. To brush away the dark moments of the afternoon, he needed to be with Hazel at the time they'd arranged, because if he arrived late, she might become sufficiently annoyed to remember her mother's advice.

'Eggs and bacon, since it's Sunday?' Kay asked, as Dean entered the kitchen.

'Yes, please, if you're offering a truce on the cholesterol front.'

'Then would you like to make the coffee and toast?'

He brought the coffee machine out of one of the wall cupboards, unscrewed the top, filled the base with water, the holder with ground coffee, screwed the top back on, and put the machine on one of the back burners of the stove.

She crossed to the refrigerator, returned with two eggs and a pack of back-bacon rashers; she poured oil into a frying pan.

'Is Leo up?' he asked.

'Awake and engrossed in one of his computer games.'

'I wonder if it's a good idea for him to spend so much time with them?'

'Depends which psychologist you listen to. And before I forget – Betty has asked us to a meal.'

He cut two slices of bread and dropped them into the toaster. 'You remembered a previous engagement?'

'I did not.'

'But George has become such a boor after a second drink.'

'Many men manage that even before their first.'

'Present company excepted?'

She smiled.

Her smiles often reminded him of their first meeting. He had always disliked cocktail parties – talking to people one didn't particularly want to know about things one wasn't particularly interested in – but had gone to one the Gibsons had given as much out of a sense of duty as because he had had nothing better to do. The centre of attraction had been a curvaceous blonde dressed in a costume that drew women's scorn and men's attention, yet his interest had been in a brunette obviously less than enthralled by what a man with an unkempt beard had to tell her. He'd interrupted the conversation and introduced himself with an easy insouciance normally foreign to him. After the beard had moved on, searching for someone more alive to his genius, Kay had smiled and told him he'd saved her from a lecture on thwarted art. Why did one woman cast a spell when another did not? Even the poets could not answer the question. That first meeting had left him entrapped – not because Kay was stunningly beautiful: gently waving, light-brown hair, dark-brown eyes that often mirrored her emotions, a jaunty, retroussé nose, a smile that could raise the sun, melded into attractive features, but not ones that might launch a thousand ships. Perhaps from the beginning he had instinctively appreciated her honesty, warmth, loyalty...

'What's dropped you into a brown study?'

she asked, as she cracked two eggs into the frying pan.

'Remembering the night I first met you at the Gibsons' party.'

'Regretful memories this early in the day?'

'A crude attempt at fishing for a compliment!'

'One has to use crude bait when the fish has become too satiated to bite ... What's your plan for the morning?'

'I've a spot of work to finish and then how about a pub lunch?'

'Excellent suggestion. And if we go to the Green Dragon, they genuinely do cater for kids ... Is the toast ready for your eggs?'

'Damn! I didn't remove it from the toaster when it popped up and now it's probably soggy.'

'You should keep your mind on what you're doing.'

'And not recall the second-most-enchanting night of my life?'

'What was the first?'

'I have to spell that out?'

She smiled again. 'Being a man, no. It won't matter if the toast is soggy, will it, since you always break the yolks on to it?'

'Women always twist logic to suit their

own ends.' He buttered the two pieces of toast, passed the plate to her. She used a slice to put an egg and rasher of bacon on each, handed back the plate.

They always had breakfast in the dining room, although there was a small eating area in the kitchen. As she was fond of reminding him, he was a traditionalist; or, she would sometimes add, perhaps more a stick-in-the-mud.

He dusted the eggs with salt and pepper from the wooden mills.

'Can't you leave your work at the office, Jerome? I don't like to see you working at home when you should be relaxing.'

'We've secured new clients on the understanding that their projects are completed a couple of days after we've explained to them what they want. They're a big concern and their contract's worth a great deal in kudos as well as cash, so we're pulling out all the stops.'

'Is Tom pulling out a single one?'

'The prime task of the senior partner is to convince himself that everyone else is working harder than he.'

She put a packet of Ryvita, plate, knife, butter and lime marmalade on the table, then sat opposite him. 'I had a chat with Mother yesterday when you were at the shoot. She sounded rather miserable, which is hardly surprising since it's coming up to the anniversary of Father's death. I wondered if we could soon go up and stay with her for a weekend to try and cheer her up? She loves seeing Leo.'

'Why not, the moment I'm on top of the work? It would be good to have a short break.'

'Then make certain you do.' She buttered a piece of Ryvita, decided she'd been too generous and scraped some butter off, added marmalade. As she was about to eat, there was a distant shout; she dropped the Ryvita and hurried out of the dining room.

As she returned and sat, he said, 'What was the trouble?'

'The play station had gone wrong.'

'Did you manage to get it going again?'

'My offer to help was rejected out of hand. I'd only make things far worse.'

'Leo's probably right: the electronic age is for his generation, not ours.'

Tudor left the CID Escort and walked towards the garden gate. Kingslee Farm was

44

the kind of home Hazel lived in in her dreams. She had a love of the past and would always have chosen crooked walls, oak beams, low ceilings and small rooms, rather than the convenience of a modern house. Three weeks before, they'd been passing an antique shop and she had seen through the window a seventeenth-century refectory table and thought this would make the perfect wedding present; when she'd learned the price, sadly she'd accepted she didn't know anyone nearly rich enough to consider giving such a present. For his part, he'd been astounded there might be someone willing to pay a small fortune for a table on which the woodworm, as well as humans, had dined well. This difference in their preferred choice of lifestyles might have caused tensions had it not been certain she was unlikely ever to be able to enjoy hers.

He opened the wrought-iron gate, walked along the brick path around the corner of the house and up to the small porch set at right angles to the house, rang the bell and waited. There was still colour in the large, well-tended garden and clearly either one or other of the Deans was a keen gardener, or they employed someone. He heard the inner door open, turned back, and through the glass-panelled outer door saw Dean step across to open it. 'Mr Dean?'

'Yes?' It was both answer and question.

'Detective Constable Tudor, local CID. I'm hoping you'll be able to answer a few questions.'

'Just so long as we can leave by twelve thirty – we're going out. Come on in and get out of the wind, which has a real bite in it today.'

He went through the porch into the triangular hall – the ancient builders had had queer ideas.

'We'll go in here,' Dean said.

The sitting room matched Tudor's expectations: the massive central beam was so low he had to duck his head under it to cross to a chair; the very large fireplace, with small recesses on either side, wasted a great deal of space; the walls were very uneven.

'I was warned someone would want to talk to me, but didn't expect it to happen on a Sunday,' Dean said, as he sat. 'But, of course, I was forgetting your job's a three-hundred-and-sixty-five-day one.'

'It's that all right,' Tudor said with feeling.

He should have been off duty, but Ted, always one of the awkward squad, had reported sick. Hazel had registered her annoyance.

The door opened and Kay looked into the room. 'Leo told me someone was here.'

'Detective Constable Tudor has to ask about yesterday, but he's promised not to hold us back from leaving in good time,' Dean said.

She greeted Tudor.

He stood. 'Morning, Mrs Dean.'

'Would you like some coffee or tea?'

'Coffee would be great.'

'I'll make some.' She closed the door.

Tudor sat. If one had to work another's turn on a Sunday, it eased the pain to meet friendliness rather than open or covert antagonism. 'I'll make it as quick as I can, Mr Dean, so I reckon it'll be best if you tell me about the morning and I pick up on any questions I need to ask.' He brought out his notebook, searched for the pen which should have been in another pocket, but wasn't.

'Shall I get you something to write with?'

'I'd be grateful for a pen.' Pencil was frowned upon because if one were both

47

skilled and careful, it was very difficult to say for certain whether there had been an erasure.

Dean left the room.

Tudor was surprised to find himself thinking that perhaps the past had given the room a mellow charm. Did one really want constantly to bang one's head on a beam? he asked himself.

Dean returned and passed across a ballpoint pen. 'Do you want me to start when I arrived at the keeper's cottage or at the second stand?'

'From the beginning, if you don't mind.'

Dean was not stopped until he began to describe the second stand.

'Nothing unusual had happened until then; you'd not seen anyone messing around in the woods?'

'No. There was nothing to suggest anyone was hiding in the undergrowth.'

'So would you say that whoever fired the fatal shot could not be blamed?'

There was a silence.

'So what are you saying, Mr Dean?'

'The ground rises in front of the guns and the beat was well under way. In those circumstances, I would not call it safe to shoot at a crossing rabbit.'

'So whoever fired the shot was dangerously careless?'

'I'd call his action that; someone else might judge differently.'

'Do you know who did fire the fatal shot?'

'If you mean, can I be certain? – no.'

'But it sounds as if you have a good idea of who it was?'

'A possible idea.'

'You're reluctant to name names?'

'I am,' Dean answered, speaking forcefully. 'As I've just suggested, I may think I know who it was, but as I didn't see him fire the shot, I could be coming to the wrong conclusion.'

'I understand what you're saying. So perhaps you'll tell me what you did see and leave us to draw the conclusions.'

Dean explained his reasons for regarding Vaillant as an unsafe shot who had little idea of etiquette in the shooting field.

Kay returned to the room, carrying a tray. He stood, took the tray from her and held it for Tudor to help himself to sugar, milk and a chocolate digestive biscuit.

After a short period of stilted conversation, Tudor said, 'If you'd finish telling me about what happened, Mr Dean, I'll get out from under your feet.' He half-expected Kay to leave, but it became clear she was not going to – wanted to hear what her husband said, he judged.

'We went to our pegs,' Dean said, 'and not long afterwards two pigeons came over. I judged them out of range, but the gun on my left fired and missed; they were followed by a hen, also missed. I had a couple of cock pheasants. Then a rabbit scuttled along, parallel with the ride, some ten to fifteen feet into the woods. There was a shot on my left and the man appeared out of the brambles and collapsed.'

'Then the next gun, who was the Frenchman, must have shot him?'

'I was looking up for birds and so didn't see what actually happened.'

'But the shot definitely came from your left?'

'Yes.'

'Could it have been one of the guns beyond the Frenchman who fired?'

'The lie of the land is such, I'd say it was impossible for either of them to have hit the victim.'

'Then I'm not certain why you have any

doubts, Mr Dean?'

'Because,' Kay said, 'my husband is very reluctant to name someone as guilty when he can't be a hundred per cent certain he is.'

'Very understandable,' Tudor said, thinking that Dean was being overgenerously fair-minded.

Ten minutes later Dean accompanied Tudor to the front door, then returned to the sitting room.

'You had to tell him,' Kay said.

'I know.'

'But it was difficult?'

'Bloody difficult.'

'A hangover from no-sneaking school days.'

'As you suggest.'

She stood. 'We must get organized. OK to leave here in a quarter of an hour?'

'Fine. Just one thing: can you explain to Leo before we go that one does not make remarks of a personal nature when in a restaurant? I'd rather not again suffer the embarrassment of hearing him describe the lady at the next table as even more wrinkly than Aunt Dorothy.'

Five

Naylor swore as he tried to tear open the covering of the stomach lozenge – he should not have had a second egg at breakfast. He picked up a pencil and used the point of the lead to force a break in the plastic; by pulling on either side of this, he was finally able to rip open the cover, extract the red lozenge, put it into his mouth and chew, hoping his stomach would soon cease to bubble.

Tudor, satisfied he could now continue, said, 'I've spoken to Mr Dean and Mr Torrents, sir.'

Naylor subdued a belch.

'I don't think there's much room for doubt.'

'When someone tells me that, I know there's a bloody roomful of doubt, if one has the intelligence to look.'

'Both Dean and Torrents, in their own way, describe Baron Vaillant as an unsafe shot.'

'What do you mean, "in their own way"?'

'Dean was reluctant to be specific; Torrents said straight out that Vaillant wasn't safe with a child's popgun.' Tudor laughed. 'Some character! The build of a heavyweight, a voice like a foghorn, and swearing like a trooper ... I could just see him as a pirate captain, a patch over one eye, shouting for a bottle of rum.'

'It would help if you stuck to your job instead of imagining a load of nonsense. You confirmed Dean was on Vaillant's right, Torrents on his left?' He stared down at the sketch in front of him.

'When facing the woods, yes.'

'Somewhat ambiguous since, according to this sketch, there are woods in front and behind.'

'The woods from which the birds were due to fly on that beat, sir.'

'Have you checked whether Torrents could see Vaillant from where he stood?'

'He couldn't.'

'Then neither of the other guns could have shot Hopkins?'

53

'Almost certainly not. There's the lie of the land, for one thing. And there's a belt of rhododendron bushes between where they stood and the bramble patch, and if theirs had been the fatal shot, there would be pellet damage to the leaves, but there isn't any sign of that.'

'You're saying it had to be Baron Vaillant?'

'It couldn't have been Mr Torrents and almost certainly wasn't Mr Dean.'

'Why not?'

'He's a very safe gun.'

'You reckon yourself to be a good judge of that?'

'No, sir. I asked one or two other people for their impressions of the guns and they all agreed, he was really safe.'

'Safe guns can make mistakes.'

'As elementary as shooting low at a rabbit on rising land when the beaters are approaching?'

'How do I know what goes on in such exalted circles ... When's the PM?'

'This afternoon.'

'Maybe that can give us a definite direction of shot, but I doubt it ... Who the hell is this Frenchman?'

'Baron Louis Vaillant...'

'I know his goddamn name. What I'm saying is, use your imagination and tell me why he's so important?'

'Is he?'

'When the Assistant Chief Constable rings and wants to know how things are, with particular reference to a Baron Vaillant, you know the Frog isn't a pimp running toms in ...What's the name of the tom area in Paris?'

'Pigalle?'

'Could be.'

There was a silence.

'We'll have to double-check everything,' Naylor said finally. 'With the ACC interested, we're under the bloody spotlight.'

Dean looked through the window of his office on the fourth, and top, floor of the brick-and-glass building, known locally as Patten's Folly. The sky was a dirty grey, the rain was constant, the wind was rising – a day to send people leafing through travel brochures and day-dreaming.

He fiddled with a pencil. He was still troubled about whether, the previous morning, he had been justified in making it obvious to the detective that he believed Vaillant had fired the fatal shot. After all, his judgement

55

was, at least in part, based on Vaillant's previous behaviour; as he had stressed, he had not seen Vaillant fire that shot ... When he'd expressed his worry to Kay, she had forcefully called him illogical. He had been asked to tell the police what he had seen and heard and he had done no more than that; to have withheld anything would have been wrong. The police would make their own judgements on the facts...

His thoughts were interrupted as a gust of wind suddenly drummed the rain against the window. It occurred to him that had the weather been like this on Saturday, the shoot would have been cancelled because in heavy rain the birds flew badly. If it had been cancelled, Hopkins would not have been killed. The weather, over which humans had no control, often decided between life and death with all the indifference of a god of war.

He dropped the pencil, opened a folder and began to check the details of the proposed project. Thankfully, unlike the law, successful advertising was not very concerned with facts.

Six

'Chez Chateaubriand' was at the northern end of Trethick Street, almost within sight of the Houses of Parliament. The restaurant was owned and run by a Cypriot, who had learned that most English people judged the quality of what they ate by its cost, and prospered accordingly.

As Sewell replaced spoon and fork on the plate, the tip of his tongue slid across his upper lip in search of any stray splash of cream. Once his tongue was under cover, he said, 'I'm delighted you were able to come and have a snack.'

'And I'm delighted there's something you want, since it's saved my having to eat at the dreary place near the office.'

Rourke, Sewell thought, really should have learned that one's thoughts must always be divorced from one's tongue. 'You'll have a

57

liqueur?' He didn't wait for an answer, called the waiter over with a gesture of his pudgy right forefinger. After Rourke had said what he would like, he ordered Benedictine, Bisquit Dubouche and cigars. As the waiter left, he said, 'I seem to remember someone wrote that a woman is only a woman, but a good cigar is better.'

'Is a smoke. Kipling.'

'Was he unhappily married? Those words would seem to suggest he was.'

'All I can tell you about his matrimonial affairs is that he and his brother-in-law heartily disliked each other.'

'A not infrequent occurrence. I, however, am fortunate in that I am on excellent terms with Florence's brother. We have many of the same interests.'

'Do you allow different interests from anyone?'

The inference annoyed Sewell, but his round, pudgy face retained an air of good humour.

The wine waiter returned with their liqueurs, the assistant head waiter with a box of cigars; he cut the cigars and struck non-safety matches.

Sewell waited until the waiters were out of

earshot, then said casually, 'I imagine you've read about the animal rights activist who intended to interrupt a shoot on Saturday and was unfortunately shot.'

'No. There's not been time to do more than skim through the headlines for the past few days because of the work.'

'He was hiding in a large clump of brambles and it seems his intention was to appear suddenly and scatter the birds and so spoil the sport for the guns. Someone shot low and hit him.'

'Justifiable homicide.'

Sewell smiled, even though he thought the remark to be in bad taste; death was not to be laughed at when one reached a certain age. 'The person who fired the fatal shot has not yet been positively identified, even though there can be little doubt who it must have been.'

'Interesting, if somewhat elliptical.' Rourke drew on his cigar, released the smoke slowly. 'I presume your telling me this is the reason for my being here. What I don't understand is why you're interested in a fatality in the shooting field.'

'The police report makes it clear it was an accident.'

'And no doubt equally clearly that it was a bloody careless accident.'

'There is no evidence of carelessness.'

'If someone's shot in the field, there's been carelessness, full stop.'

'The gun could not possibly have known the victim was in the clump of brambles.'

'He must have been shooting low and without a clear field of fire – two of the most deadly faults, as you well know. So suppose you tell me where all this is leading?'

Sewell tapped ash from his cigar into an ashtray. 'My father was always annoyed if one did that, but I never learned why; he always allowed the ash just to fall off.'

'No doubt your mother had little difficulty in explaining why she was annoyed when he did so and the ash fell on the furniture ... Come on, gird your loins and try to forgo your delight in prevarication.'

After a while, Sewell said, 'The police naturally took statements from all the guns immediately after the incident and have questioned them since; the man they believe to be guilty on the evidence vehemently denies having fired the shot.'

'Of course. But if there's sufficient evidence – and if the police admit a degree of certainty, there probably is – where's the problem?'

'He suffers from an inordinate self-esteem and if it were shown he had killed the man, he would be publicly exposed as a liar and an incompetent and careless shot.'

'What's wrong with that?'

'Should he feel humiliated, there would almost certainly be political and financial consequences.'

'Which are ...?'

'You must understand I'm speaking in the strictest confidence.'

'You're speaking in such confidence I've no idea what you're really saying.'

'He is French.'

'No surprise there. A Frenchman will always shoot a running pheasant provided only that it's not going too quickly.'

'He is politically very highly connected, being both a friend of, and an adviser to, the President.'

'Not on shooting, I trust?'

'This is not a matter for jest,' Sewell said testily. 'Do you recognize the name of Sparkson and Tennant?'

'I think I've come across it at some time or other, but it doesn't say anything to me right now.'

'They're a large firm in the electronics field that carries out considerable work for the British government. Likewise, the French firm of Pensec and their government. For many months, discussions between the two firms have been in progress concerning an amalgamation. Politically this would make good sense, not only because so much of the work of both firms is connected with defence, but also because it would demonstrate our determination to march with Europe.'

'Out of step, I trust?'

Sewell's thin lips momentarily tightened – his only sign of annoyance. 'Financially, it could be said to make equal, or even better sense. It has been projected that in very few years, if on its own, neither firm will be in a position to meet either the technical or productive competition from the States; if amalgamated, able to eliminate all unnecessary duplication and spend more on research and development, they would be well able to provide solid competition. However, at the last moment, we have learned that Pensec has, without reference to us but with the approval of their government, been discussing a similar proposal with a German firm. Were this to take place, it is projected that Sparkson and Tennant would be unable to meet the competition, not only from the States, but also from Europe. It would eventually be forced to close, resulting in massive redundancies and the loss of cutting-edge research, so necessary in our age of technology.' Sewell began to twist the stem of his glass between thumb and forefinger. 'The Frenchman, having been to Germany, is here to speak to the British firm and perhaps the British government, after which he will decide which amalgamation should be pursued. The best opinion is that, whatever his decision, it will be followed. I do not have to spell out what that decision will be, should he be humiliated at British hands.'

'You're not suggesting a decision this important might rest on personal pique?'

Sewell tried not to show his surprise at such naivety.

'Who is this Frenchman?'

Sewell released the glass, and said in so low a voice that Rourke could only just hear him: 'Baron Vaillant.'

'I seem to recognize the name.'

63

'He would undoubtedly be mortified if you did not.'

'I think it was one of his ancestors who, at the Battle of Waterloo, ran away.'

'A canard.'

'What is the labyrinthine reason for your telling me all this?'

'Because the man's death was an accident, there will be no criminal charge.'

'If there was gross negligence, he might have been guilty of manslaughter.'

'The police accept there was no reason he could, or should, have suspected someone was hiding in the brambles.'

'To shoot low when beaters are advancing...'

'It was not a beater who was killed. An Initial Case Review will not be sent to the CPS. There will, however, have to be an inquest. But since there is no suspicion of murder or manslaughter, this can be held without a jury; and further, as the coroner is not empowered to decide who killed the victim, he can call witnesses to testify to events, but not to determine who fired the fatal shot.'

'And you'd like the witnesses to be anyone but Baron Vaillant?'

Sewell did not answer.

'You're attempting to manipulate the law.'

'Nonsense! There can be no manipulation when the law accepts no crime has been committed.'

'How can the law do that until it is determined in court whether or not there was gross negligence?'

'You are complicating matters without reason. All one is asking is that one witness is not called before the coroner – a witness whose evidence is quite unnecessary, yet whose appearance in the box might well cause him to reach a decision that would be financially and politically harmful to our country.'

'I think it will be best if I don't understand what you've been saying.'

'You are within your rights to understand or not understand and no one could criticize you for that. Indeed, some might applaud your readiness to sacrifice yourself in the name of principle.' Sewell tapped his cigar over the ashtray. 'Despite my father's admonition, I always tap. Perhaps that is the mark of filial protest we are all said to host.' He drew on the cigar, exhaled. 'I was very sorry to learn you'd failed to gain the promotion you deserved. As someone wrote, "Uncommon ability is as likely to be a disadvantage as an advantage." '

'John Gates. And it was "more likely".'

'You are a mine of information.'

'You spoke of sacrifice in the name of principle. What are you telling me in that corkscrew way of yours?'

Sewell chuckled. 'No one is likely ever to admire your tact!' He raised his glass and drank, replaced the glass on the table. 'Have you heard about poor old Digby?'

'No.'

'He died last night.'

'A merciful release for his wife.'

'Indeed, one might perhaps venture to say that ... Now that his position will no longer be held open in the hope of his recovery, there is a vacancy that must be filled. Of course, it can be no secret that you must be the favoured candidate – you have achieved considerable success as acting head of the department.'

'I've learned a candidate can be ill-favoured as easily as well-favoured.'

'In a world dedicated to conformity, the independent mind always faces difficulties. However, a strong recommendation from a senior officer would surely make certain that this time you were not disappointed.'

'Something I imagine I am hardly likely to receive.'

'An independent mind will always identify advantages a pedestrian mind does not. For instance, it can judge the likely benefit of engineering an obligation to return a favour.'

Rourke stared at Sewell, then past his right shoulder. His voice was low and harsh. 'Are you suggesting what I think you are?'

'Being unable to enter your mind, I cannot answer.'

'Are you offering me a bribe?'

'My dear Charles,' Sewell huffed, 'that is quite unworthy of you. Surely you have known me long enough to judge I would never betray the principles by which I live? I was merely suggesting you consider all possibilities, since I have found over the years that if one does that, often one will find gold amongst the dross.'

'As far as I'm concerned, what you've just uncovered is all dross.'

'I'm sorry you feel the need to speak as you have. However, I'm quite certain you didn't mean to sound insulting, so the matter is forgotten. Now, how goes the time?' Sewell pulled back the cuff of his expertly tailored coat. 'I fear I must be on my way; life becomes ever more stressful.' He called for the bill, paid with a credit card. As he stood, he said, 'When life becomes too confused, I console myself with the words Swinburne wrote: "The true success is to labour." '

'Stevenson.'

'Can you not leave me with even the faintest shadow of erudition?'

He stood, threaded a way between the tables, overweight and awkward in movement – to most, a pompous man of little consequence; to a few, a Machiavellian bastard. He came to a halt on the pavement. 'Now to discover if it is correct that there is always a plenitude of taxis until one wants one ... Can I give you a lift somewhere?'

'I'll walk to the tube.'

'I admire such energy. By the way, according to a whisper from on high, the position of head of your department is to be upgraded, meaning a not inconsiderable increase of salary and pension rights.' An oncoming taxi came into sight and he waved it down. 'Common perceptions are almost always fallacious.' He climbed into the back; the taxi drove away.

Rourke began to walk. He had been bitterly disappointed when he had failed to gain promotion the previous year, in part because of dented *amour propre*, but far more because the increased salary would have enabled him to provide a little more colour in his disabled daughter's life.

He had been brought up to honour honour, to understand that whilst those who served the law were honest, there would be justice, and where there was justice, there was freedom; conversely, dishonesty threatened justice and therefore freedom ... Yet how would he be subverting justice? If the police were satisfied no offence had been committed, there was no crime. If those witnesses who were called at the inquest provided the evidence to determine the circumstances of the death and since the coroner was legally prevented from determining who had fired the fatal shot, where could there be harm in ensuring one witness was not on the list of those to be called?

He reached the tube station, went down to the southbound platform in time to see a train leave. He stared unseeingly at the posters on the far side of the track. His daughter's life could never become normal, but added income would ensure Jane's burden of looking after her could be lightened by employing help. If a witness was not called who, strictly speaking, should have been, that could be said to be wrong. Yet if the witness's evidence would establish nothing of consequence, but would cause considerable harm, how great a wrong? Surely a minor transgression could be pragmatically justified when it must benefit many at no expense to anyone?

Seven

Dean drove into the garage, switched off lights and engine, left the car, walked round to the garden gate, opened it. From the field to his right, on the other side of the small orchard and the road, came the ugly cries of a bulling cow; several pigeons flew overhead, their forms blurred by the growing darkness, and they were followed by an even less distinct wisp of starlings, their passage marked by the rush of wings.

He stepped into the porch, switched on the overhead light, took his key from his pocket and unlocked the inner door; as he opened that, Kay came out of the sitting room.

She kissed him. 'For once, you're not too late!'

'I managed to clear my desk in good time because the weekly conference finished early; with Tom away, we didn't have to listen to endless reminiscences.'

'Is he ever going to retire?'

He took off his lightweight overcoat and hung it up. 'All the time he's at the office, he doesn't have to be at home with Iris.'

'And they say men aren't as bitchy as women ... Ready for a drink?'

'I'll change first.'

'Then I'll have it poured out when you come down. Gin and tonic?'

'Please. Why the blissful silence? Is Leo out?'

'In his room, zonking Martians.'

'Again? When I was his age...'

'You buried your head in twopenny dreadfuls to the despair of your father, who said you ought to be improving your mind, not anaesthetizing it.'

'How would you know how I spent my time?'

'Your mother told me not so long ago, after she heard you complaining about Leo's leisure habits.'

'Mothers should keep memories of their young in cold storage.' He crossed to the stairs, climbed them to the short, narrow landing, turned into their bedroom, the largest of four; the beams in here had in some previous century been attacked by woodworm, which had failed to reach the heart of the iron-hard oak.

He took off his suit and tie – no dressing down at Hartley & Catchpool: the chairman, Tom Evans, lived in a past era – put on polo-neck sweater and flannels, and returned downstairs to the sitting room, where there was a small wood fire in the wrought-iron basket in the middle of the inglenook fireplace.

'The room was warm,' Kay said, 'but I decided it would be more cheerful.' She handed him a glass. 'Ralph told me this afternoon he can get us a load of last year's cut wood that will have dried out.'

'Supplied by his cousin, no doubt?'

'I'm not certain.'

'We'd better find out before we order.'

'I don't think the cousin's as big a rogue as you make out.'

'You, my love, have the disarming fault of not being able to think evil of anyone.'

'Which is better than thinking evil of everyone.'

'More Christian, surely, but inclined to prove expensive.' He raised his glass. 'Here's to us.'

As they drank, there came the crash of an upstairs door being slammed shut. 'Have you ever explained to Leo that a door doesn't have to be closed hard enough to hold back the Martians?' he asked.

'Several times.'

Leo pounded downstairs, rushed into the room and excitedly announced he had qualified as a top gun; then, scornfully, had to explain what that meant. He crossed to the television and switched it on, used the zapper to call up cartoons, increased the volume.

'Not so loud, dear,' Kay said.

'But I can't hear.'

'Then we'll buy you some earphones. We may be able to find some that won't make you look too odd when you wear them.'

Leo decided he could hear the programme with the sound lowered.

They ate their normal supper of toast, cheese, and salad, and drank half a bottle of Rioja between them. As Kay began to clear up the plates, she said, 'I've completely forgotten to tell you that in the local paper there's a report on the inquest. It's not long, but your name appears and there's a refer- ence to the fact that you're a partner in the firm.'

'I wonder if that will please our chairman – free publicity almost makes him smile – or displease him, that a partner should be mentioned in downbeat circumstances?'

She put plates, cutlery, cheese dish, and toast rack on a tray, which he carried through to the kitchen. 'Coffee?' she asked.

'Yes, please ... Where is the *Gazette*?'

'By the telephone. I was reading it when Laura phoned.'

'How is she?'

'As scatter-brained as ever. Wanted to know if we were going to the Rushtons next week. I had to remind her the invitation was for Tuesday week.'

'With Frank as stolid as a statue, I do wonder what their life is like behind closed doors.'

'Don't you think she's just the kind of person he should have married?'

'On the principle that contrasting charac- ters make for happy marriages?'

'That he needed someone to teach him not to take life too seriously. Haven't you noticed how he smiles when she giggles because she knows she's said or done something stupid?'

'He smiles *continuously*? ... So you left the *Gazette* in the hall?'

'Unless it was somewhere else.'

'Laura would understand your logic.' He stepped into the hall and picked up the newspaper that had been wedged between telephone and wall, on the top of the oak corner cupboard. If it was true that every wife had at least one annoying habit, hers was to scrumple a newspaper before he had had time to read it.

'Page six, I think,' she called out.

He read the single-column report. It recorded that he had been standing almost directly in front of the patch of brambles from which the injured man had appeared. He smoothed out the newspaper as far as was possible, folded it and put it down. 'I'm still curious as to why the Frenchman wasn't called to give evidence when it's certain he fired the shot.'

'Perhaps he was able to claim diplomatic immunity.'

'I didn't gain the impression that he was a diplomat – in fact, judging from his manner, he certainly isn't. Whatever, it's all over and done with, thank God! The sight of the poor devil standing up, clutching his stomach ... The only good thing is, he wasn't married and there's no grieving wife or fatherless kids.'

'I sometimes...' She stopped.

'What?'

'Nothing.'

'Confess your innermost thoughts.'

'I sometimes frighten myself imagining you driving off in the morning and not returning and a policeman arriving to tell me you've had a terrible car accident because some drunken fool came round a corner on the wrong side of the road.' She turned off the hob under the coffee machine. 'I don't know how I could cope.'

He put his arm around her and held her against himself. 'You'd cope because under that gentle exterior, there's steel.'

She gripped his hand, then released him. 'Steel can buckle.'

As he stepped back, he silently acknowledged he had his own fears, because life often seemed to resent too much happiness.

The post was left in the porch, on the ledge of the small window. Dean picked up the four letters, tried to judge their contents from a quick look at the envelopes, paused to stare through the window at the garden, as much of the sloping field as was visible, the line of oak trees, and the woods. It was one of those days when one needed to remember that summers had not been abolished; a dark, overcast sky promised more rain and the sodden land seemed to bear a miasma of gloom.

He returned into the hall.

'Is there anything from Jenny?' Kay asked, from the head of the stairs.

'No. Are you expecting to hear from her?'

'She promised she'd let me know how Basil is. I'll have to ring her this evening to find out. Who is the mail from?'

'Two junk, one from the Cartwrights, and one from an unknown source.'

'Where are they now?'

He rearranged the letters, studied the top one. 'The postmark's Cape Town.'

'Do you think they ever get tired of travelling around the world?'

'Not judging by their actions. Isn't it less than three months since they were cruising off Alaska?'

The bracket clock in the sitting room

struck the half-hour and, as the door was open, the chimes were audible in the hall.

'I'd better get a move on or I'll be late at the office,' he said.

'With all the overtime you do, so what?'

'Not the style of logic that appeals to Tom. I'll have a quick bite...'

'You'll have a proper breakfast.' She came down the stairs. 'And whilst I'm cooking it, you can tell me what Helen has to say.'

'Don't you mean, "has written"?'

'You're becoming ever more pedantic.'

'Flatterer!'

She passed him and went into the kitchen; he followed her and used a knife to open the first letter in order not to damage the stamps which, together with dozens of others, would be sent to a charity. 'Helen writes that the ship is very comfortable, the crew very helpful, the other passengers very interesting. In other words, they're having a lousy voyage, but aren't going to give us the pleasure of knowing that.'

'Talk about speaking evil of other people! ... Who else has written?'

'A child, judging by the name and address being in somewhat wonky capitals.'

'Then it's from my godchild, at long last.'

'It's addressed to me and the postmark's Redford.'

'Maybe I am just not going to get a thank-you letter from him. The young seem to have lost the habit of writing them ... One rasher of bacon or two?'

'Greed says two.'

She dropped the rashers into the saucepan. He again used the knife to open the envelope, withdrew a folded single sheet of notepaper, and opened it. 'What the hell!'

'An unexpected bill?'

'A message made by cutting words out of a newspaper.'

The toaster pinged and two pieces of toast appeared; she picked them out and put them in the rack, dropped in two more slices of bread. 'It's a joke?'

'I suppose so.'

His tone caused her to turn and stare at him.

'Probably Jasper after a third bottle of Beaujolais.'

'What's it say?'

'Nonsense.'

'Let me see it.'

'Not worth the effort.'

'You know it's not from Jasper, don't you?'

'Why would I suggest it is if I know it isn't?'

'Because for some reason you think it'll worry me. I want to read it.' She held out her hand.

He hesitated, passed it to her. In addition to the printed words, there was one in handwritten capital letters. 'You have got yours coming to you, you murder bastard.'

'Oh, my God!'

'It's just someone's sick idea of humour.'

'Of course it isn't,' she said fiercely. 'Who do we know brainless enough to send something like this? It isn't a joke.'

'It can't be anything else.'

'You must take this to the police.'

'And have them laugh me out of the building?'

'Shit!'

She swore so seldom, he momentarily thought fear had unnerved her. 'Look, I'm sure you don't need to worry...'

'Yes, I do. I've burned the bacon.'

He laughed.

'I'd like a word with someone,' Dean said, as he stood at the counter in the front room of Divisional HQ and spoke to a bearded PC.

'Your name, please?'

'Dean.'

'Right, Mr Dean. So what would this be about?'

'I've received a letter that's a little worrying because it seems to be threatening me.'

'Then if you'd like to wait over there, I'll get someone to speak to you.'

He crossed to a small recess in which four could sit in comfort, five in discomfort; on the stained table were a couple of ancient magazines and several advisory pamphlets addressed to the public. He picked up a magazine and leafed through it; either the cartoons weren't amusing or his humour was out of date. He looked at his watch. Already late for work. Yet as Kay was always keen to point out, he did considerable overtime, which surely left him entitled to take time off when he needed to; his problem was a conscience that could confuse logic and duty.

Tudor came through a doorway, saw him, and crossed to where he sat. 'Hullo, again, Mr Dean.'

Dean stood, returned the greeting.

'I gather you want a word about a letter you've received, so if you'd like to come through.'

He followed Tudor down a corridor, which smelled musty, and into an interview room that possessed all the charm of an ancient railway station. He sat on one side of the table, Tudor on the other, brought the letter from his pocket and passed it across.

Tudor opened the envelope, brought out the sheet of paper, unfolded it, and read. He looked up. 'You don't think this might be a joke?'

'I doubt it is.'

'The postmark's Redford. Presumably you have a number of friends who live in or near here; might not one of them be trying to have so-called fun at your expense?'

'I can't think of anyone with quite such a warped sense of humour.'

'Has anything happened in the near past that might cause someone to bear a grudge against you?'

'Not to my knowledge.'

'You've not had a bitter argument with anyone?'

'No.'

'There's been nothing unusual happening in your life?'

'Only the inquest.'

Tudor picked up the letter and reread it. 'You just can't think of anything that might have caused someone to send you this letter?'

'No.'

'Then, to be frank, it's going to be difficult to take the matter any further.'

'Naturally, I appreciate that. In fact, if left to myself, I'd have torn the letter up and chucked it into the WPB, but my wife insisted I come and show it to you. She ... is rather easily alarmed.'

'Very understandable. I think the best thing is for you to leave this letter with me so that I can have some further thoughts. In the meantime, if you should think of someone who might have sent this, or if anything else unusual happens, be in touch.'

Dean stood. 'Thanks for your help.' His tone made it clear he was not being sarcastic.

Naylor stared down at the letter lying open on his desk. 'You're saying it's probably not sent by a friend with a bloody stupid sense of humour?'

'That was my initial reaction, sir, but then he reminded me he'd attended the inquest on Hopkins. Calling him a murder bastard might somehow be connected with that.'

'How?'

'The sender of the letter might think Mr Dean fired the fatal shot.'

'More likely he's one of the nutters who surfaces after every serious incident.'

'They usually claim to be the guilty party, don't they, not threaten someone?'

'When dealing with nutters, there's no such thing as "usual". Record receipt of this letter and it's decided no further investigation is warranted.'

Tudor did not move.

Naylor leaned back in his chair; because of the angle at which he was now holding his head, a double chin had become a treble one. 'Well?'

'Mr Dean says his wife is very worried.'

'Probably a hysterical woman.'

'Having met her, I doubt that.'

'You're a trained psychologist?'

'No, sir.'

'Then leave that judgement to someone who is.'

'But wouldn't it be an idea to send the letter and envelope to Forensic to find out if it can tell them anything?'

85

'Have you feathers between your ears?'

'No, sir. It's just...'

'We need extra work like a visit from the Chief Constable.'

Tudor left.

Eight

The phone rang at a quarter past eight in the evening. Dean was at a business reception given by the firm and Kay hurried into the hall, hoping to lift the receiver before the noise awoke Leo, who had been even more reluctant than usual to fall asleep.

'Is Mr Jerome Dean there?' a man asked.

She did not recognize the voice, which was coarse and muffled; the 's' was hissed. 'I'm afraid he's not at home. Can I help you?'

The man giggled.

She experienced sudden fear. 'He'll be back any minute now, so if you'd like to ring again soon...' Dean probably wouldn't be returning in under an hour, but she didn't want the caller to think she and Leo would be on their own.

'You his missus?'

'I am Mrs Dean.'

'Then it'll be you what has to get the flowers. White lilies always looks good on the coffin and—'

She slammed down the receiver. Her hands were shaking as she picked it up again and dialled. A woman answered; just audible were the sounds of several voices. 'I want to speak to—' she began.

'The office is shut.' The connexion was cut.

Panicking, she dialled again. This time, a man answered.

'I must speak to my husband, Jerome Dean. It's very urgent.'

'Hang on.'

She waited; time became elongated.

'Are you checking up if I've run off with the red-head secretary...' Dean began.

'I've just had a ghastly phone call. He said you'd be in a coffin. I don't know...'

'Steady on, my sweet. Tell me slowly what's happened.'

She did so.

'Almost certainly, some drunk.'

'He gave your name.'

'Opened a directory and chose a name at random.'

'Don't you understand? He wasn't drunk.

He sounded slimy. He was laughing at me. When I asked if I could help, he giggled because he was enjoying a perverted joke.'

Dean said, 'I'll return right away. Check all the doors and windows are fast and at the slightest hint of trouble, dial nine nine nine.'

She replaced the receiver, crossed to the stairs and hurried up them, needing to re-assure herself that Leo was unharmed.

'Will you give the words as exactly as your wife can remember them,' the PC in the operations room said over the phone.

Dean did so.

'There was no direct threat?'

'There didn't need to be, not with that letter a week or so ago. Can't you under-stand...'

'I'm sorry, Mr Dean, all I can do is record your report. Someone else will make what-ever investigations prove to be necessary. Do you have caller identification and was it switched on?'

He answered that they did, it had been switched on, but his wife had been too upset to read the number indicated.

'If there is a similar call,' said the PC, masking his weary acceptance of the public's incompetence, 'try to make a note of the caller's number.'

Dean replaced the receiver.

'What did they say?' she asked.

'Not very much. The man I spoke to will pass the information on to someone who'll investigate what happened. And will we try and read the number if there's a similar call.'

'I suppose he thought I was being hysterical. I'm not, I'm just terrified because there's someone who hates you so much.'

'It may not be quite as bad as—'

'If you'd heard him giggle, you'd know he wants to hurt you.'

'The police will find him before he can cause any harm ... How about a drink to restore confidence?'

'You think that right now a whole bottle could do that?'

'Yes?' Unwin muttered as Tudor walked into his room.

'I've just read the night log, sarge.'

'You want a signed commendation for bothering to carry out orders?'

Judging from the detective sergeant's ill temper, it might well be true that Naylor had bollocked him for lazy paperwork. With only months to go before he retired, Unwin was relaxing a little too thoroughly. 'So what's happening about the phone call to Mrs Dean?'

'What d'you mean?'

'Who's going to have a word with her and her husband?'

Unwin scratched the side of his neck. 'Have you ever suffered from an allergy?'

Yes, Tudor thought: *to ill-tempered sergeants.*

'I only have to eat half a bar of chocolate and I come out in a bloody awful rash. So what do I do?'

'Stop eating chocolate.'

'You think you're paid to be smart?'

'If I were, my salary would be double.'

'Get out.'

'Is someone talking to the Deans?'

'You think we're going to bother about finding out which of their friends is playing the fool?'

'Sarge, roughly a week ago, Mr Dean gets a letter telling him he's got it coming to him because he's a murder bastard; now, there's a phone call and a man tells Mrs Dean white lilies will look good on her husband's coffin.'

'So?'

'It can't be a sick joke. I'm sure it's for real.'

'Then there's no room for argument. It isn't.'

'That call must have terrified her.'

'Only if she hasn't the sense to realize it was a drunken friend; or maybe their friends don't have to get tight to be totally stupid.'

'As Mr Dean said—'

'I'm not wasting time over a woman who's scared by a phone call from a man who doesn't even ask if she's wearing knickers.'

'Suppose you're wrong? Suppose that call was from someone determined to waste her husband?'

'Plodding DCs don't suppose, they *do*. And you're going to follow up the request from another force for a witness statement from Taylor, who lives at...' Unwin searched amongst the papers on his desk, found the one he wanted. 'The address is on here. They want to know where he was at twenty-three hundred hours, last Friday, who he was with, what did he see, and can he identify the second man in the knife fight?'

'Has the first man been identified?'

'Yeah. In the morgue.'

Taylor, in his late twenties, head shaven, earring in the right ear, stubbled chin, dirty clothes, signed the statement that Tudor had written down and handed it back. He spoke ingratiatingly. 'Not a word of a lie.'

'Is that why it was so difficult telling me?'

'Don't be like that, Mr Tudor.'

Tudor stepped into the short, narrow hall, which smelled of something it was better not to try to identify. A door to his right was opened a few inches and someone looked out; straggling hair over that part of the face which was visible left him uncertain whether the other was a man or a woman.

He returned to the car and drove off; ten minutes later he stopped at lights. Redford to the left, Brightlee to the right. Back to the station or a word with the Deans? Unwin had made it clear that in the unlikely event of an investigation into the phone call to Mrs Dean, it would be a perfunctory one. This was not because of incompetence or indifference, but a decision enforced by reality. Police forces were underfunded, overwhelmed by paperwork, castrated by politicians, and unable to carry out their jobs as they should. Unwin had to believe it would be cost-effective to try to identify the man who had made that call before any action was taken; but how could he, when the chance of success must be small?

Tudor turned right because he had never learned how to become indifferent to other people's troubles. Ten minutes later, he drew into the yard at Kingslee Farm.

Kay met him in the porch. 'Good morning, Mr Tudor.'

He gave her full marks for remembering his name. 'Is it convenient to have a word?'

'Since I've been waiting a long time for someone to come here, it is.'

She had spoken pleasantly, but with sharp undertones; as he had previously judged: a determined nature. He stepped into the hall, followed her into the sitting room; there was no fire, but the room was warm from two radiators concealed behind oak covers.

'Can I offer you anything?' she asked. 'Coffee, tea, or a drink?'

'No, thanks.'

'Do sit.'

When they were both seated, he said, 'You received this phone call yesterday evening, just after eight?'

'Yes.'

'And you judged the speaker was threatening your husband?'

'That's hardly surprising when he told me I should be ordering flowers and white lilies would look good on the coffin.'

'He didn't directly say they were for your husband?'

'No.'

'But you presume that was who he had in mind when he talked about a coffin?'

'Of course I did,' she answered sharply. 'My husband had received that letter, so I was very worried anyway. And at the beginning, when he wanted to speak to Jerome and I asked him if I could help, he giggled. That giggle made me feel ... I don't expect you to understand.'

'His giggle convinced you he wished your husband ill?'

'He seemed to be secretly laughing because something dreadful was going to happen.'

'Did you recognize the voice?'

95

'I'm quite certain I've never heard it before.'

'Was it a rough voice?'

'More soapy and slimy.'

'Did it carry an accent – north country, estuary, local?'

'I don't think so.'

'There was nothing distinctive about it?'

'Only that he hissed his "s"s. A friend of ours who, poor man, never seems to find false teeth that fit, does the same thing. Which is why, for one wild second, I wondered if it was he. It wasn't, of course.'

'Would you judge the caller to be an educated man?'

'Not from the way he spoke. But, of course, these days education and good speech don't coincide.'

'Did he use any word or phrase that made you think he might have a special background or interest?'

She spoke quickly. 'You have to understand, I was so scared, I wasn't taking everything in; he might have said something I don't even know I heard.'

'Are you fond of white lilies?'

'Not particularly.'

'Do you grow any in the garden?'

'No. Why do you ask?'

'Because this man mentioned them.'

'Surely, because they're often regarded as funereal flowers?'

'Yet if they had been a favourite of yours, this might have suggested he knows quite a lot about you and therefore was probably an acquaintance, if not a friend.'

She gripped the arms of the chair briefly, then relaxed.

'Mrs Dean, I have to ask you this: could the man be a friend who disguised his voice in order to carry out a very stupid joke?'

'I've answered that more than once.'

'I know, but—'

'You obviously believe we have friends capable of behaving atrociously.'

'I have to consider every possibility, however absurd. Can you think of anyone who has, or might think he has, reason to hate your husband to the extent of threatening to kill him?'

'He's never been that unpleasant to anyone.'

'I'm quite sure of that, but what I'm trying to establish is if someone could have the mistaken belief that he does have such reason.'

'There isn't anyone.' She paused, then said, 'This man sent that letter, didn't he?'

'It seems likely, but we can't be certain.'

'When are you going to be certain and stop him?'

'We're doing all we can.'

'And if that proves insufficient?'

'Don't think along those lines, Mrs Dean.'

'In my shoes, you wouldn't be thinking along any others.'

He thanked her, stood. 'There is one last thing. Please try to remember to note down the number of every caller you don't immediately recognize.'

'You think the man is going to ring again?'

'There is the possibility or perhaps the probability that he will, because he's no intention of carrying out his threats, but wants to frighten you and your husband. So get on to us immediately if he does – I'll give you a number that will put you straight through to CID.' He reached into his inside coat pocket and brought out a card, handed this to her. 'I'm sure we'll soon sort out the trouble so that there'll be no further need for you to worry.'

As he walked along the brick path and opened the gate, he named himself a hypocrite. In truth, he wasn't sure they would ever have the chance to identify the unknown tormentor, let alone do so quickly.

Mrs Wraight prided herself on having a forthright nature; there were many who would have preferred the word 'domineering'. 'For heaven's sake, Sean, not there.'

Tudor hastily picked up from the kidney-shaped writing table the vase in which were the six golden chrysanthemums he had bought on his way to Aston Avenue.

'Has no one taught you that water ruins good furniture?'

'Sorry, Mrs W.'

As he looked around the overcrowded room for somewhere safe to place the vase, Hazel, certain her mother could not see her face, smiled mockingly at him. He crossed to the fireplace and put the vase down on the imitation-marble mantelpiece. He returned to the table and visually inspected it. 'There's not a drop of water on it,' he said, as he straightened up.

'Undoubtedly, more by luck than judgement.' Mrs Wraight liked the last word.

He looked at his watch, spoke to Hazel. 'I think we ought to be moving.'

'Where are you going?' Mrs Wraight asked.

'I don't think we've decided yet.'

Hazel said, 'Didn't you say it would be fun to try Ricky's?'

'Never mentioned the place.' He spoke hurriedly. Ricky's had recently been in the news because the pole dancers had shown unusually imaginative dedication to their job; Mrs Wraight might have read the report in the *Gazette*. 'How about a curry supper?'

'If you do have one, try not to eat anything with fenugreek in it,' Mrs Wraight said. 'It is so long-lasting.'

He hoped not all daughters grew to resemble their mothers.

When they were seated in his car, he said, 'Why on earth mention Ricky's?'

There was laughter in Hazel's voice. 'I wanted to see how you'd react.'

'I hope you were satisfied.'

She put an arm around his shoulder, leaned across to kiss him quickly on the cheek. 'You'd been in a brown study ever since you arrived, so I had to do something to lighten things up.'

'If your mother knew what went on at Ricky's and thought I'd taken you there, she'd ban me from the house.'

'Mum's not nearly as starchy as you seem to think.'

That was news to him.

She nibbled the lobe of his ear. 'It was such fun seeing you all embarrassed.'

He started the engine. 'One bad turn deserves another.'

She drew back and settled in her seat. 'What's that supposed to mean?'

'Later on, I'm going to enjoy myself finding out just how embarrassed you can become.'

The restaurant was small, cheerful, and reasonably cheap; an ambience of sorts was provided by large framed photographs of Bollywood stars, temple dancers, and a snake charmer.

The waiter cleared their dishes and Tudor asked for the bill; as the waiter left, Hazel said, 'Come on back.'

'How's that?'

'Come back to me from wherever you are. You've been staring into space as if you were in a trance. What is the matter? Have I said or done something that's upset you?'

'Of course not.'

'Aren't you feeling very well?'

'I'm fine.'

'You won't tell me?'

'Not here.'

The waiter brought the bill and Tudor paid it; he and Hazel left the restaurant and walked along the wide High Street and down a side road to his parked car.

'Now,' she said, as he settled behind the wheel, 'you're going to explain why you've been as companionable as a corpse.'

'I'm sorry. I've been trying to remember something and can't, and that's been driving me nuts.'

'Obviously something far more important than me.'

'Nothing is more important than you.'

'Then try to remember that another time.'

He kissed her. 'A woman's worried silly because her husband's being threatened and neither of them knows why or by whom. I'm certain I've recently learned something that might help to answer the problem, but when I try to remember what that is, my mind goes blank. It's so bloody frustrating to see a nice person scared and not to be able to do something to help her.'

She kissed him. 'One reason I love you, my

darling, is because you care so much about other people.'

Later, in fact, he remembered. But he did not tell her so, because the circumstances were such that she would have expected his mind to be on other matters.

Nine

Naylor said testily, 'You went to Mrs Dean's house and questioned her yesterday morning?'

'Yes, guv,' Tudor answered as he stood in front of the desk.

'I thought the case was frozen unless or until there was fresh evidence?'

'Yes. But the thing is—'

'Did Sergeant Unwin tell you to question her?'

'Not exactly.'

'I imagine a straight negative would be more accurate.' Naylor spoke slowly. 'Clearly, I have to remind you that for a team to be successful – and every department is, or should be, a team – there has to be discipline. Discipline means that when an order is given, it is obeyed; when a decision is reached, it is observed...'

The lecture was long and filled with clichés.

'Sir,' said Tudor finally, 'I reckon I've uncovered further evidence which means the case should be active.'

'Because of what you learned from speaking to Mrs Dean?'

'Yes. She told me—'

'Presumably, you have already reported to Sergeant Unwin?'

Tudor spoke rapidly to forestall a lecture on the chain of command. 'I asked her to describe the voice of the man who made the threatening phone call. She didn't notice any regional accent, or use of words or phrases that might indicate a particular background, but she did say he tended to speak his "s"s with a hiss, rather as if he had badly fitting false teeth.'

'That is the further evidence?'

'On its own, I know, it's obviously useless. But when I'd spoken to Lynch to tell him his partner was seriously ill in hospital, I'd noticed he hissed his "s"s.'

'You're suggesting that fact is sufficient to hold him responsible for the letter and the phone call?'

'It seems a possibility.'

'Why?'

'The relationship between him and Hopkins was obviously an intense one. In which case, he may be so emotionally shattered by Hopkins's death he has decided to gain revenge.'

'Revenge for what?'

'The shooting of Hopkins.'

'I fail to follow the logic. Dean did not shoot Hopkins.'

'I reckon there's reason for Lynch to think he did.'

'Which is ...?'

'In the report in the *Gazette*, the names of only two of the guns were given, one of which was Dean's. And the wording of the article made it clear Dean was pretty well opposite Hopkins when Hopkins was shot. What's more likely than that, in those circumstances, Lynch should think he shot Hopkins?'

'The evidence Dean gave at the inquest should refute any such possibility.'

'Not all the evidence was printed and, in any case, one needed to understand the nuances. To someone in the depth of despair, too emotionally upset to think logically, who has no idea what the powers of the coroner are, nuances are unrecognizable. Revenge is usually taken quickly; here, there's been no direct action, just a threatening letter and, six days later, a phone call that might well have been dismissed as having been made by someone playing the fool but for that letter. The man understands that the more slowly he acts, the less specific his threats, the greater the fear; I've only spoken to Lynch that once, but I'd say he might well appreciate this.'

Naylor began to drum on the desk with his fingers. 'Supposition and untested judgement.'

'Which is why I think we should start testing it, sir.'

'How?'

'Send the letter to the lab and ask them to name what newspaper the words were cut from; find out which paper Lynch usually reads; ask for a check on telephone records to find out if he called the Deans yesterday evening; question him pointedly, because if he begins to think we suspect him, he's sufficiently highly strung to get into a lather – fear could unnerve him, as it has Mrs Dean.'

Naylor did not speak for a while and the

only sounds were the tapping of his fingers and the muffled noise from the traffic. 'I'd like time to think on it.'

'Sir.' Tudor turned away, then back. 'Have you any idea why the Frenchman wasn't called at the inquest?'

'No.'

'It's strange that he wasn't. Do you think there could be some sharp reason behind his absence?'

Naylor stopped tapping. 'Sergeant Unwin said the other day that you have a very active imagination. I don't think he meant that as a compliment.'

The phone rang. Kay, her expression suddenly strained, lowered the magazine she had been reading and stared at the door of the sitting room.

'I'll get it.' Dean stood, left.

She increased the volume of the baby-alarm receiver. She heard the rhythmic sounds of sleep, yet the certainty Leo was safe failed to lessen her fears.

As Dean stepped back into the room, she said, her voice shrill, 'Who was it?'

'Janice.' He closed the door. 'She wants one of us to tell the vicar she's sorry, but she can't do the flowers in church on Sunday.'

'Why not?'

'She and Ben have had an invitation for the weekend.'

'If one promises to do something, one does it unless it becomes impossible.'

'For Janice, it did, the moment the invitation was issued.' He put a log on the fire, then sat.

'She's no sense of responsibility.'

'But a great appreciation of where pleasure's to be found.'

'Why do you always stand up for her?'

'Do I? Perhaps it's because she often makes me laugh.'

'She's totally selfish.'

'Which can amuse.'

'You're talking nonsense.'

'And you, sweet, are talking like someone living on her nerves.'

'That surprises you?'

'It makes me worry. Things have been difficult – bloody difficult and unnerving; but the police will soon identify the half-wit who's causing all the trouble.'

'If they can even be bothered to try. You know what happened when Alfred's place was burgled. He phoned the police, but no one ever turned up at the house. And when he complained, he was told police resources had to be concentrated on cases that involved physical harm. So why should they worry about us until...' She did not finish.

'If that held true, the detective would not have come here yesterday and spoken to you.'

'Probably that was just to make us think someone was doing something.'

'That wasn't your opinion yesterday.'

'Wasn't it?'

'You told me he'd been supportive. You...'

'Well?'

'You're letting yourself worry far too much.'

'That's wonderful! You're threatened by some madman and tell me I'm not to worry. For God's sake, how do you expect me to forget?'

He stood, crossed to her chair, put his hands on her shoulders. 'I know it's rough, but the police will identify the maniac and make certain he doesn't do us any harm.'

She reached up and gripped his wrists. 'If anything happened to you, I don't think I could go on.'

He knew sudden emotional ice. Her words

reminded him that sooner or later one of them would die and the survivor would have to carry on.

Typically, Tudor thought as he drove, Unwin had expressed his resentment by snidely ordering him to question Lynch shortly before he had been about to go off duty. The detective sergeant resented the fact that he'd spoken directly to the detective inspector about his theory that Lynch might be the man who was threatening Dean. As he'd left the CID general room and made his way down the stairs – the lift was still out of action – he'd considered the possibility of leaving the questioning of Lynch until the next day and reporting to Unwin that Lynch had not been at home. But then, as he'd walked from the building to his car, he'd remembered how scared Mrs Dean had been and he had decided that if there was the slightest chance of helping banish that fear, he must take it. Ted Allright would call him a daft sod – become emotionally involved in a case and one was bound to make a fool of oneself.

He found a parking space in Well Road, locked the car, walked along to number 2.

He rang the bell and 'Home, Sweet Home' chimed.

The door opened; Lynch looked at him for a second or two without recognition, then became visibly uneasy.

'Sorry to bother you,' he said.

'As if you give a shit!' Lynch said, with weak anger.

'Is it all right if I come in and have a word?' Lynch's lifestyle did not arouse in him the contempt it did in some members of the force; nevertheless, even on the briefest acquaintance, he experienced an instinctive dislike of the other.

'A word about what?'

'What's happened.'

'Keith's been murdered, that's what's happened.'

'It was a tragic accident.'

'That's what it's being called because they're rich.'

'The law doesn't work like that.'

'Then why ain't he been arrested?'

'Hasn't who been arrested?'

'Who murdered him.'

'It'll be best if I come in and we talk inside.'

'There ain't nothing to talk about. He's

dead.' Lynch's eyes filled with tears.

Tudor, showing the crude authority that did not come naturally to him, stepped inside and Lynch instinctively moved to his left. 'Shall we go in there?' Tudor entered the front room. On his previous visit, the room had been clean and tidy; now there was disorder: on the glass-topped coffee table were dirty plates, cutlery and an empty can of beer, on the floor a newspaper, magazines were strewn across the settee and a small pile of discs had collapsed on top of the CD player.

Tudor sat. The newspaper was near enough for him to identify it as a copy of the *Guardian*. On the mantelpiece above the blocked-in fireplace was a framed photograph of Hopkins and black ribbon had been loosely pleated around it.

'So what d'you want?' Lynch asked shrilly, as he remained standing in the centre of the room.

'Just a bit of a chat; nothing dramatic.' A friendly approach might gain a response whereas an aggressive one would scare Lynch and cause him to become weakly, but stubbornly, uncooperative. 'I'll be as brief as possible, but it'll still take time, so why not sit?'

Lynch hesitated, then removed some magazines and sat.

'I'm here because we have a problem and think you may be able to help us with it.'

'I don't know nothing.'

'That's not strictly true, is it? You think you know who killed Mr Hopkins.'

'I couldn't when I wasn't there.'

'Perhaps you've spoken to one of the beaters or keepers who was.'

'Don't know any of 'em.'

'Still, I expect you read the *Redford Gazette*?'

Lynch hesitated. 'Sometimes,' he finally said.

'Did you see it a week ago?'

'Can't remember.'

'There was a report on the inquest into Mr Hopkins's death. If you read that...'

'I didn't.'

'I thought you just said you couldn't remember whether you'd seen last week's edition?'

'I'd know if I'd read about ... about...' He gulped.

'What was written in that article might well have led you to believe Mr Dean fired the fatal shot.'

'I didn't read it.'

'It's a natural reaction to hurt someone who's hurt you. So if you believe Mr Dean was responsible for killing your partner, you'd probably want to make him suffer as you are suffering, wouldn't you?'

'No.'

'You weren't so fond of your partner to think of revenge?'

Lynch leaned forward and covered his face with his hands as he began to sob.

'You must understand,' Tudor said quietly, 'Mr Dean did not fire the shot that killed your partner, so there was no reason to send that letter.'

Lynch uncovered his face and tried to regain his self control. 'What ... what letter?'

'The one you sent to Mr Dean, which you composed by cutting words out of a newspaper. You called him a "murder bastard" and threatened he would get what was coming to him.'

'I didn't send nothing.'

'Because you couldn't find the word "murdering" you had to be content with "murder" and because "bastard" was equally absent, you had to write it out in pencil...'

'I didn't.'

'The experts will be able to prove who wrote that word. They're going to name you.'

'They can't prove nothing when it's capital letters.'

'Did I mention capitals? I don't think I did, so how do you know that capitals were used? A question easily answered: you wrote the word.'

Lynch's fear was obvious.

'Ironically, you're incorrect in your belief. Capitals can be sufficiently individual to identify the writer. And in this case, they almost certainly will be because – or have you forgotten? – you also wrote capitals on the envelope ... There's something you now need to consider very carefully. Courts show sympathy for someone who clearly has been under great emotional distress and who confesses, thus saving time, trouble and expense; but, inevitably, much of that sympathy vanishes when the accused continues to deny his guilt despite the overwhelming evidence against him. So it has to be in your interests to admit you sent the letter and made the phone call, since then you might well merely be bound over to keep the peace rather than receive a custodial sentence.'

'I didn't write the letter, didn't phone no one.'

'You phoned the Deans' house on Monday and told Mrs Dean she should order flowers, and white lilies looked good on a coffin.'

'It wasn't me.'

'I've been wondering, why white lilies? And it occurred to me that perhaps those are what you had placed on your partner's coffin. Am I right?'

'I ain't saying.'

'I'm sure the undertakers will remember, so I'll ask them. What firm was in charge of the funeral arrangements?'

'I don't remember.'

'I'll ask around. Now, one more thing: I want you to write the word "bastard" and Mr Dean's name and address in capital letters on a piece of paper.'

'I won't.'

'Why not?'

'I won't,' he said wildly for the second time.

'Don't you understand that if you didn't send Mr Dean the letter, the quickest way of proving that is to write out the words so they can be compared and shown to be totally dissimilar to those on the envelope and in the threatening message?'

'I ain't doing it.'

'As you wish.' Tudor stood. 'You have my word that Mr Dean did not fire the shot that killed your companion, so you're trying to gain revenge on the wrong man. Wouldn't you agree that that's not only irrational, it's also ruining the life of someone who is completely innocent?'

'He murdered my Keith,' Lynch shouted. Tears trickled down his cheeks; there was spittle around his lips.

Tudor left, knowing sympathy for Lynch even while cursing him for a fool.

As Tudor hurried from the car park to the jeweller's through heavy rain, he regretted his earlier decision not to bother with a mackintosh because the day was going to remain fine; as a weather forecaster, he'd make a good dustman.

Hazel's birthday was in a fortnight's time. Had he won the lottery, he would have bought her an ancient manor house stuffed full of antique furniture, because true love was always eager to offer a sacrifice; not having won anything, he hoped he could afford the silver Lakeland terrier he had seen in the jeweller's window a week before. Hazel had always wanted a living Lakeland, but her mother did not like dogs – they smelled and had objectionable habits.

The assistant, with the supercilious superiority considered essential by those engaged in luxury trades, pointed out that the dog was a Border terrier, not a Lakeland; he added with satisfaction, when asked if a Lakeland could be obtained inside two weeks, that it would take at least a month for the order to be processed. Tudor silently swore before it occurred to him to pick up the model and check if the name of the breed was marked; it was only recorded on the label. The two breeds were, as far as he knew, similar, and the model was attractive but not detailed, so if he removed the label and told Hazel it was a Lakeland, a Lakeland it would be. And he wouldn't be lying, since the slight misrepresentation was intended to give pleasure.

He arrived twenty minutes late at Divisional HQ.

'Nice to see you so early,' Curran said

jovially.

'Blame my enthusiasm for work.' He removed his mackintosh, shook off some of the rain, hung it on one of the pegs at the side of the noticeboard, briefly looked at the jumble of papers pinned to that – calls for the identification of ringed heads in photographs, duty rotas, memoranda from County HQ, appeals for more hands to join the rugger club – then crossed to his desk. 'What's making waves this morning?' he asked, as he sat.

'A couple of muggings late last night outside the bingo hall, a hit-and-run in Larkstone – victim didn't need to be hospitalized – two domestics, neither serious, and a break-in at our beloved mayor's palatial home.'

'Was much nicked?'

'Very little, and he says that what was taken wasn't valuable.'

'A pity.'

'What's he ever done, apart from living the life of Riley at our expense, to get up your nose?'

'I stopped him for careless driving when I was in uniform. He swore I was insolent and reported me. The super told me to leave him alone unless I had half a dozen witnesses ready to swear I never called him a stupid bastard.'

'I read his daughter's gone into modelling.'

'Then she can't look like her mother or she's modelling outsize.' Tudor picked up and read a duplicated notice that had been left on his desk. C division's clear-up rate had fallen again and now was the second-lowest in the county force. All officers must put greater and more efficient effort into their work, ensuring better figures for the next month ... A guarantee, he thought, that in the coming days old lags when arrested would be persuaded to admit to a series of petty crimes of which they knew nothing until then, none of sufficient consequence to increase their likely sentences.

Unwin looked into the room. 'Want a word with you, John.' His round face disappeared.

Tudor wondered yet again why the detective sergeant sometimes called him by an incorrect Christian name. Because of his professed dislike for the Irish? There was Scots and Welsh blood in the Tudors, but no Irish; his mother had just liked the name Sean.

Unwin appeared more lumpy than usual as he sat slumped in the chair behind his desk. 'I'm sure you've written your report, being conscientious, but I can't find it, no doubt due to my incompetence. Whereabouts on my desk did you leave it?' His sarcasm was always laboured.

'I was about to write it, sarge. Would you like a résumé first?'

'That wouldn't be too much trouble?'

'Lynch denies everything, but he's our man all right. He believes Dean fired the fatal shot and so is determined to make his life hell.'

'Proof?'

'He was nervous to begin with, soon in a sweat, and ended up as good as admitting he believed Dean was responsible.'

'I asked for proof.'

'He reads the *Redford Gazette*, but says he can't remember if he saw the issue of the eleventh in which the report of the inquest appeared; a check with newsagents just might be able to prod his memory. He knew the word "bastard" had been written in capitals although I hadn't told him; he's convinced capital letters can't be used to identify the writer, but as an insurance he refused to write that, or Mr Dean's name and address, in capital letters, even though I pointed out the advantage of doing something that would help prove his innocence. It's odds on Hopkins was buried with white lilies on his coffin, which is why Lynch referred to them in his phone call.'

'And ...?'

'That's it.'

'Then you're about as far from presenting a case as you can get.'

'But now I'm certain he's our man, I'll extend inquiries. I'll check with undertakers to find out—'

'You think the guv'nor will agree to you swanning about when there's no certainty Lynch had anything to do with the letter or the phone call?'

'But as I said—'

'And I'm saying, you'll forget that and get your feet into this.' Unwin picked up one of the five files on the desk.

Tudor stepped forward to take the file. 'What about the Deans?'

'What about them?'

'She's convinced her husband's about to be murdered.'

'That's known as a wife living in hope.'

'If you'd seen the state she's in, you wouldn't say something so bloody silly.'

'And if you don't want your next assessment written in red ink, you'll keep your tongue a sight cooler when you're talking to me.'

Tudor left. Lacking hard evidence, Unwin could claim he was justified in putting the Dean case back on hold; it needed an ability to appreciate vicarious fear to understand why the investigation should continue.

Ten

Kay was coming downstairs, having made certain Leo was sleeping soundly, when the brick came through the window. 'My God, what's happened?' she called out as she tried to guess what Dean had dropped and broken. When there was no answer, she continued to the bottom of the stairs in a rush, scared of what she might find in the sitting room – Dean unconscious, blood pumping out of a torn artery? She could raise disaster between two blinks of an eyelid.

Dean was not unconscious, bleeding to death. He stood by the window, looking out, as cold, damp air, driven through the shattered right-hand pane of glass by a rising wind, ruffled his hair. He turned and answered her unasked question as she came to a halt underneath the central beam.

'That's been thrown in.' He pointed at a brick, around which a sheet of paper had been secured with a thick elastic band. Careful to avoid the slivers of glass, he picked up the brick, removed the elastic band and paper, and put the brick down on the windowsill. He opened the sheet of paper. The message had been composed from words cut out of a newspaper: 'One death earn another'. Knowing how shocked Kay would be by the words, he momentarily wondered how to prevent her knowing them, but accepted that to try to prevent this would merely exacerbate her fears. 'That's one way of delivering a message. Breaking news, one could say.'

'It's the same person?' Her voice was high.

'I imagine it has to be.'

'What does it say?'

'A short ungrammatical and illogical comment. "One death earn another".'

'What are we going to do?'

'I'll try to find something to board up the window before we freeze to death...'

'For God's sake, you know what I mean.'

'All we can do is report what's happened.'

'Tell the police they've got to do something or he'll kill you.'

126

He went forward, careless of crunching glass, to hug her. 'He doesn't intend to kill me or he'd have found a more lethal weapon than a brick. His aim is to scare us.'

'Why?'

'Heaven may know; I don't.' He released her. He went through to the hall, crossed to the phone, lifted the receiver, dialled 999.

A woman asked him which emergency service he needed. When the connexion to the police was made, he reported what had happened. His listener seemed unimpressed and suggested the culprit was almost certainly a youth. When he tried to explain why this was unlikely, he was told that the incident would be logged.

He returned to the sitting room; Kay was staring at the broken window, apparently oblivious to the cold draught. 'Are they coming?' she asked shrilly.

'Maybe.'

'What d'you mean?'

'The man I spoke to obviously didn't regard the matter as priority. In a way, I suppose he's right. Whoever threw the brick will have left as quickly as he could.'

'Are you saying the police aren't going to do anything?'

'My guess is, there won't be anyone here until the morning.'

'God Almighty! Don't they give a damn what happens to us? We can't go on like this.'

He tried to comfort her.

Naylor read the faxed report from the ops room at County HQ. 'I imagine you've seen this?'

'Yes, sir,' Unwin replied.

'Have you sent someone to speak to Dean?'

'Not yet.'

'Why not?'

'With the Larksberry robbery and GBH last night, I reckoned Dean's case had to be left until there was more time to deal with it.'

Naylor's silence denoted an acceptance of that fact; his following question showed that the threats to the Deans were no longer in his mind. 'Have the staff come up with a total loss yet?'

'Not officially; unofficially, it'll reach six figures.'

'Shit!' The greater the loss, the more media interest; the more media interest, the greater the demand that those guilty be arrested, and then success would be expected, failure a black, black mark. Naylor wanted to retire as deputy chief constable of a county force, or higher, not a DI who had failed to make even DCI. 'Has the lead of the taxi driver any depth?'

'Doesn't look like it.'

'Then we've not much to go on.'

Nothing, Unwin thought, already reconciled to failure.

Tudor returned to Divisional HQ cold, tired and hungry. He reported to Unwin. 'I've questioned everyone and it's a case of seven witnesses, eight different versions of events.'

'Been wasting your time, then,' Unwin observed.

'Since no one's taught me how to weave moonbeams.'

'What's that?' The detective sergeant was clearly in one of his dourer moods.

'Sarge, I've been questioning them until I know almost as much about their jobs as they do, but learned nothing – and if any of them was feeding the villains, I'm a Dutchman.'

'Double Dutchman.'

Tudor dutifully laughed.

'The guv'nor's shouting loud.'

'He would be, seeing the villains helped themselves to close to half a million.'

'Where d'you learn that?'

'One of the staff told me just before I left.'

'You'd better pass the figure on to the guv'nor.'

'And make his evening so cheerful he has everyone working all night?'

'It wasn't given to you officially?'

'No.'

'Best leave things as is, then.'

Tudor crossed to the door.

'By the way, your friends received a visit last night.'

'My friends?'

'The Deans.'

'What kind of visit?'

'A brick with a message wrapped around it was thrown through a window.'

'What was the message?'

'"Murder earns murder", or something like that.'

'Christ! That'll have knocked her sideways. What's moving?'

'Someone will be along there when there's time.'

'Are you saying no one's talked to them yet? Sarge, with Lynch as mentally unstable as a March hare on vodka, anything can happen.'

'What are we supposed to do when there isn't any hard proof it's him? And one can argue from the evidence that it isn't. There was no phone call on his line to the Deans on the Monday.'

'How do we know that for fact?'

'The report's through from BT.'

Nice of Unwin to tell him. 'That doesn't mean he didn't use a mobile or a public phone. The mobile companies will have to...'

'They won't have to do anything. You reckon we can begin to justify a request that would take time and effort?'

'Sarge, I don't care what the evidence isn't, Lynch is our target. I've told Mrs Dean that the man is only trying to frighten them, to ease her fears, but it could well be much more serious than that. We have to do everything possible to nail him before he does kill her husband. Surely a man's life...'

'You're beginning to sound like you've taken a shine to the missus.'

Tudor thought of several things to say, but managed not to say them.

Tudor sat in his car and tried to persuade himself it was ridiculous to consider acting on his own account again. If his seniors decided the case had too low a priority to be pursued for the moment, it was surely up to him to accept their decision? Yet he could not forget how scared Mrs Dean had been, or ignore the certainty that if she had reason to believe nothing was being done to ensure the safety of her husband, her fright could only increase ... He started the engine, backed, drove up to the exit and then turned right on to the road. He could 'hear' Unwin sarcastically calling him a Holy Joe.

He arrived at Kingslee Farm as dusk turned into dark, with over half the sky clear and stars appearing. A moment after he rang the front-door bell, Dean stepped into the porch, recognized him, unlocked and opened the outer door. As Tudor entered the hall, he heard the sound of music coming through the partially opened doorway of the sitting room; he recognized the music without being able to name its source with any certainty: *Bohème*, *Traviata*, *Turandot*?

132

'Who is it?' Kay called out.

'Detective Constable Tudor,' Dean answered. He turned and was about to open the door fully when it was pushed from inside and Kay, framed in the doorway, faced Tudor and said, 'You've finally managed to get here!'

'I'm afraid we've several very serious cases in hand...' Tudor began.

'And the murder of my husband isn't serious?'

'The threatened murder,' Dean said lightly, trying to lessen the resentment her words, and tone, might have caused. 'We've been enjoying a drink; can we offer you something?'

'No, thanks.'

'Then come on in.'

The fire-basket was filled and the wood was burning well; firelight danced on the walls of the deeply inset fireplace.

'Do sit.' Dean noticed Tudor was looking at the drawn curtains. 'We managed to get the window reglazed this morning.' He sat. 'Something of a miracle, really, since having a minor repair carried out has become almost as difficult as counting hens' teeth.'

'Have you arrested someone yet?' Kay

demanded.

'No, Mrs Dean,' Tudor answered.

'Have you even been bothered to try to find out who's threatening my husband?'

'We're doing all we can.'

'Which clearly isn't very much.'

'There's always the problem of finding proof that will be accepted in a court of law. So we may suspect someone, but cannot...'

'You know who it is?'

'We are continuing our investigation.'

'Is that supposed to be an answer?'

'I'm afraid it's the only one I can give.' He continued quickly, hoping to prevent further questions provoked by his inadvisable mention of a suspect. 'Will you tell me exactly what happened last night?'

'My wife was upstairs,' Dean said. 'I was here, watching television, when a brick came through the window. At first I was too startled to understand what had happened, then I saw the brick on the floor and all the broken glass.'

'What time was this?'

'About a quarter past nine.'

'What did you do next?'

'Went over to the window and pulled back the curtains, thinking the brick had been thrown by kids and I might be able to catch sight of someone.'

'Did you succeed?'

'There was no one.'

'Were you aware of hearing anything unusual from outside the house before the brick was thrown?'

'No. But then I was listening to the television.'

'When you looked through the broken window, you saw nobody, but did you have any impression, however indistinct, of movement?'

'Only a car, which was driving off rapidly.'

'From your yard?'

'No. If it had come into the yard, the outside lights on the garage would have come on.'

'Could you judge which direction the car was going in?'

'Towards the T-junction.'

'I don't suppose you've any idea of what kind of a car it was?'

'None whatsoever.'

'Do you have the message that was wrapped around the brick?'

Dean stood, crossed to the small Georgian lowboy on which stood a vase of flowers on a mat.

Despite the mat, Tudor thought, Mrs Wraight would have had something to say about that.

Dean picked up a transparent plastic bag, handed it to Tudor. 'I reckoned I shouldn't handle the paper directly, but I'm afraid that was only after I'd first removed it from the brick and read it.'

'Most people would never have thought of taking any precaution, Mr Dean.' Tudor read the message, composed from words cut out of a newspaper; this time, none had had to be handwritten. 'I'll take this for the lab to examine.'

'And if they don't learn anything from it?' Kay demanded.

'We'll keep searching, Mrs Dean.'

'So my only hope is that you succeed in definitely identifying this lunatic and having the proof to arrest him before he murders my husband?'

'As I said before, it's unlikely it's his intention to commit murder; that would call for more courage than he has...'

'It would be courageous to kill my husband?'

'I'm saying it always requires a perverted

courage to plan to kill someone and carry it out, rather than to kill someone in a flash of anger. So this man's motive is to frighten you...'

'Which he is succeeding in doing all too well.'

'I hope...' Tudor became silent, certain his words would sound either condescending or stupid. He stood. 'We'll be doing everything we possibly can, Mrs Dean, even if it might not seem that way to you.'

'We know that,' Dean said.

Was Dean more trusting than his wife, Tudor wondered as he walked to his car, or merely more diplomatic?

He settled behind the wheel, checked the time. Did he now return home, warmed by the knowledge he had played the part of a knight in shining armour? He drove out of the yard and turned left. The trouble with being a knight in shining armour was that one's task was not completed until it was certain the heroine was saved.

The headlights picked out the first of four small bungalows on the right of the road. He braked to a halt, left the car and with the aid of a torch made his way up the gravel path to the front door; even in torchlight, it was clear this needed repainting. He knocked and there was a demand to know who he was. He answered. The door was opened to the length of a security chain and he held his opened warrant card in the light. The door was closed sufficiently for the chain to be released, then was fully opened by an elderly man, who was taking his weight on a walking stick. 'Sorry to bother you this late, but you might be able to help me. Were you here last night?'

'Of course I was.'

'Would you have been in the garden or on the road at around a quarter past nine?'

'Of course I wasn't.'

Tudor persevered. 'Did you happen to hear a car go by, being driven very quickly, at about that time?'

'All the cars is going too fast. Don't bother about anyone else. It ain't safe...'

Tudor listened with an ever-lessening patience to the perils of the road that the speaker had endured. When there was a pause, he thanked the other, returned to his car. Wasn't it just common sense to accept he was not going to learn anything; to think he might was not optimism but stupidity? Yet a small, silent voice told him that to give up now would be the act of a quitter.

At the fourth bungalow, the middle-aged Mrs Harkness said, Yes, she had been outside yesterday evening, despite the concern of her husband, because Old Bert was doing poorly and she'd taken him some beef tea, which she knew was an old-fashioned remedy but was as good as anything one could buy in the chemist's even when one was suffering from...

He politely listened to a catalogue of the ills to which mankind was subject before he said, 'Do you think you were out at around a quarter past nine?'

'Can't rightly say. I mean, I wasn't watching time that close.'

'Did many cars pass when you were walking along the road?'

'Two, three maybe. It's not busy at night. And as I tell Dad when he doesn't like me going out on me own, I always have a torch, so when I hear a car coming, I step up on to the grass verge and shine it at my feet so as the driver knows I'm there.'

'Did one of the cars go past you very quickly?'

'Funny you should say that. I heard this one coming up behind and it sounded like it was going so quickly, I was a bit scared. So I waved the torch up and down my legs.' She chuckled. 'Likely the driver thought I was suggesting something!'

Doubtful, Tudor thought. 'This car was being driven more quickly than most?'

'It most certainly was. And when it went round the corner, I heard the tyres squealing.'

'Could you tell what make of car it was or whether it was a saloon, hatchback or estate?'

'In the dark?'

'I know! ... I don't suppose there was anything unusual about it that you noticed?'

'Just how fast it was going.'

It was time for a touch of PR. 'That's important. You've been very helpful.'

'Glad to give a hand. All I have to do now is explain to Dad what you wanted. Don't think so clear as he used to.'

He began to walk back towards the wooden gate at the end of the small front garden.

'I don't suppose it's anything,' she called out.

He stopped and turned.

'One of the red lights was blinking on and off, quite quick. Does it mean something special, like a police car?'

'I don't think so. That could be very useful, so thanks again.'

He resumed his walk. It sounded as if the car had a malfunctioning rear light, so it might be worth checking Lynch's car. But ask to examine it and Lynch must realize that to give permission to do so could be dangerous, and he would refuse. On the evidence available, a compulsory order would not be granted and even if it were, by the time it could be served, the faulty rear light might well have been repaired. He opened the gate and stepped out on to the road. For a sharp mind, there was always more than one way of skinning a cat.

There was grey sky, damping air, and a forecast of heavy showers by mid-afternoon – a day to make even an optimist wonder if the sun had vanished.

Tudor handed the message that had been on the brick thrown through the Deans' window to a PC who had been detailed to take several items to the county forensic laboratory; that done, and the PC away, he spoke to Unwin.

'I had a word with Mr and Mrs Dean

yesterday evening, sarge...'

'Did you? After I'd told you the case was frozen? Then you're going to learn...'

'In my own time.'

Unwin stared at him, his disbelieving astonishment obvious. 'You're trying to con me that you questioned them outside working hours?'

'That's the picture.'

'I suggest it's one of them surrealistic pictures and you're a bloody poor liar.'

'I arrived at their house well after six and they'll corroborate that.'

Unwin fidgeted with a pimple on the side of his thick neck. Since he had been careful never to work unnecessarily, he was disturbed by something he could not understand.

'They gave me the paper that had been wrapped around the brick and since time is of the essence, I've sent it off to the lab to see if they can make anything out of it.'

Authority for the request for a laboratory examination should have been given by an officer of the rank of sergeant or higher. But Unwin, accepting he had made a mistake in calling Tudor a bloody poor liar, did not raise the point. (Rule 71b, *The Police Officer's Handbook*: 'No officer will at any time address someone junior in rank to himself in terms which are likely to cause offence'.)

'Apart from the message, the Deans were not able to raise any fresh evidence, but there's the chance they were able to provide the lead to a lead – a long shot, but worth following up.'

Unwin rubbed the pimple too hard and winced.

'So I'll see if it gets anywhere.'

Tudor returned to the CID general room, spoke briefly to Lee, the only other DC present, sat and phoned Lodge. 'It's Sean. How's the world treating you?'

'With more kicks than kisses.'

'Would you like to do me a favour?'

'No.'

'You owe me one. During your next turn, call at number two, Well Road ... You know where that is?'

'You think I arrived in the division last week?'

'And tell Edgar Lynch you want to inspect his car.'

'On what grounds?'

'Think of something. Tell him he was reported for driving like Jehu.'

'Who?'

'Never mind. Check the rear lights and see if one of them's literally on the blink.'

'Then what?'

'Thank him for his willing assistance.'

'What's this in aid of?'

'Good relations.'

'If you suffered the ones I'm lumbered with, you'd know they only exist in fairy stories.'

Eleven

Lodge rang as Tudor was working at a computer, detailing an arrest on an RB 216 form and cursing every time he hit a wrong key.

'Just finished our turn, so I thought I'd give you a bell. We had a butcher's at Lynch's car, a two-year-old Fiesta, and told him he'd been reported by a civilian for careless driving; seemed to send him spare.'

'An emotional type. What about the lights?'

'A loose connexion in the offside rear one, so when the car's moving, it flickers.'

'Make that an official report so it's on the books.'

'How do I explain to the sarge when he asks what the hell's it all about?'

'You'll think of something.'

Tudor replaced the phone. His immediate

reaction to the news was to tell Unwin that here was the evidence to identify Lynch as having thrown the brick through the window of the Deans' house; a moment's thought detailed the scorn with which such an assertion would be received. Where was the proof to rebut the possibility that this was a coincidence? Wasn't it inevitable that dozens of cars were driving around with rear lights blinking because of faulty electrical connections? How was it to be determined that the behaviour of the blinking red light Mrs Harkness had seen was exactly similar to the behaviour of the blinking rear light of Lynch's car? If Lynch denied he had been driving his car near Kingslee Farm on Wednesday night at around nine fifteen, where was the evidence to prove he was lying? Even if it was his car and he had been driving it, what evidence was there that he had thrown the brick through the window of the Deans' house? If the car had been travelling noticeably quickly, how did that prove the driver was trying to get as far away as quickly as possible? ... The problem that so often faced the police when investigating a crime was the need to provide proof that was acceptable in a court of law. Time and again, they uncovered sufficient evidence to convince themselves they had identified the person responsible for the crime, but insufficient to provide a legal case against him. The difference between street and court proof enabled many a villain to live a happy and contented life.

The phone rang as Kay was about to break two eggs into the frying pan – she had decided that for once they would both enjoy a cooked breakfast even though it was not a Sunday. She put the eggs down on the working surface and removed the frying pan from the heated ring, was about to hurry into the hall, when she heard Dean answer the call. A moment later, he came into the kitchen.

'Was it a wrong number?' she asked.

'Unfortunately, no.'

'Oh, my God! Another...'

He hastily interrupted her, realizing his words had caused unnecessary worry. 'It was Bill, wanting me to give him a hand.'

Her words were angry because of her sudden panic. 'Why does he keep asking you? Why can't he do things for himself instead of always shouting for help?'

'I made the mistake when he bought the machine on my recommendation of saying that if he ran into any problems, I'd do what I could to help.' He paused, then said slowly, 'You must try to stop panicking every time the phone rings or you'll end up a nervous wreck. The detective told us, this idiot hasn't the courage to do anything positive, so he's trying to frighten us with threats that are meaningless.'

'If the police don't know who he is, how can they judge whether he does, or doesn't, have the courage?'

'You're forgetting how the detective mentioned a suspect and then very hurriedly back-pedalled away from admitting they did have one? For my money, they have identified the bastard who's doing this to us.'

'Then why haven't they arrested him?'

'They're probably getting ready to do so.'

'And until they actually do?'

'We spike his guns. If he phones again, we laugh at him; tell him we enjoy a good joke, but his are very feeble. That'll disconcert him so much, he'll probably give up.'

She resumed cooking. 'Blast!'

'What's the problem?'

'I've forgotten to make the toast.'

148

'Then we'll have eggs on bread. Keep things ticking over while I butter a couple of slices.'

'I'm sorry.'

He looked up, the knife in his right hand held up in the air. 'Sorry for what?'

'Behaving like a jelly.'

'Like a wife who's scared for her husband, not herself.'

'And Leo. But I just can't help it.'

'Who the hell could? We're conditioned to act normally and reasonably and to expect others to do the same, so when someone acts abnormally and illogically, it's totally confusing and frightening even if he isn't really a threat.'

'I suppose ... Is the bread ready?'

'No, but it will be in a couple of seconds.' He buttered vigorously, placed a slice of bread on each plate, carried the plates across to the stove.

'I'm afraid the eggs are overcooked because of my being stupid.'

'I prefer them well done.'

'You know you like them with runny yolks.'

'When boiled and I want to dip fingers of bread, reliving my spotless youth.'

149

'Hardly spotless. Your mother says you hated washing so much she began to fear you could be hydrophobic.'

'A typical mother's exaggeration!' He judged he had managed to relieve at least some of the tension from which she was suffering. He wished he could accept his own words. The fact was, the police might well have a suspect, but until they arrested him, he remained free to pursue his senseless campaign of fear.

'Where the hell are you going?' Lee asked, as Tudor turned right.

'Well Road.'

'Why?'

'To question Lynch.'

'Who's he?'

'The man who, I'm convinced, has been threatening the Deans.'

Lee brought a pack of cigarettes out of his coat pocket, lit one. He lowered the window sufficiently to throw the spent match out – smoking was forbidden in police cars. 'Rolf says you've gone spare.'

'It takes one to know one. And coming from him, that's a compliment.' Tudor braked hard and swerved to avoid a pedestrian who had stepped out into the road without checking it was safe to do so.

'We're meant to be heading back to the station and soon the sarge is going to be shouting, Where are we?'

'Lynch is trying to put the frighteners on the Deans.'

'Since their case has been put on ice...'

'Because the guv'nor and sarge can only think of doing things by the book.'

'Might do you some good to think the same.'

'Mrs Dean is scared silly for her husband. When someone's that frightened, you have to try to help.'

'You do?'

'You're saying you wouldn't?'

'I'd like to draw my pension when I leave the force.'

'You are all that's important to yourself?'

'If that makes any sense, yes.'

Little more was said before they parked in Well Road, on the opposite side to number 2 and several houses along. Tudor switched off the engine, withdrew the key. 'Lynch isn't going to be all that easy.'

Lee had been about to open the passenger door; he kept his hand on the release catch. 'So?'

'It'll likely need pressure to loosen his tongue.'

'Are you that far round the twist?' Lee demanded angrily. 'We're here when we should be there, investigating a case that's supposed to be in the freezer, and you're talking about using persuaders?'

'Mental, not physical pressure; giving him a taste of what he's been doing to the Deans. He's rat-like sharp, but I'm certain there's a weak streak in him, so if I can make him believe that if he doesn't cough, a ticket to Dartmoor will be a bonus, he'll crack.'

'And likely he'll be complaining to authority before you've had time to think up a fiction.'

'So you're here to back me up and tell 'em I never was anything but calm and polite.'

When Lee was standing on the pavement, he addressed the privet hedge that fronted a small garden. 'I need to see a psychiatrist.'

Lynch opened the front door, recognized Tudor and instinctively made as if to shut it.

Tudor pushed it wide open. 'We're here for another word.' He stepped inside.

'You can't force your way in...'

'You invited us.'

Lee, uneasily wondering how close to disaster Tudor was prepared to go, closed the front door behind himself.

Tudor crossed to the sitting-room door and went inside. The room was, if anything, more untidy than before and the black ribbon around the framed photograph of Hopkins had slipped and was partially obscuring the face. The gas fire was full on and the air was oppressively hot and stuffy.

Tudor sat and, after a momentary hesitation, Lee did the same. Lynch remained standing in the middle of the room, trying to reject Tudor's assumption of authority in his own house, but lacking the character to do so.

'If I were you, I'd sit,' Tudor finally said. 'This is going to take time.'

Lynch sat on the edge of an armchair, as if ready to spring up and away.

'There's no need to explain why we're here because you know.'

'No, I don't.'

'Going to play stupid, are we?'

'If it's about the letter...'

'Five out of ten.'

'I told you, I don't know anything about that.'

'What a pity you will keep lying; it gets everyone so annoyed.'

'It's the truth.'

'I don't think so, Edgar. But let's talk about Wednesday.'

Lynch began to lick his upper lip, realized he was being watched and withdrew his tongue.

'Where were you on Wednesday?'

'Here.'

'All day?'

'No, of course not. I was at work.'

'So what kind of work do you do?'

'I'm a librarian.'

'That needs a lot of brains, does it?'

'I wouldn't say so.'

'Nice to find you're modest. What about after work finished? What did you do then?'

'I spent the evening watching television.'

'In between going out, you mean.'

'I was here all evening.'

'What programmes did you watch?'

'I don't remember.'

'Not surprising, since you weren't watching anything most of the time, seeing as you weren't here.'

'Hang on.'

'What for? Christmas?'

154

'I do remember now.'

'Surprise, surprise!'

'I watched a play about Charles the First.'

'Into history, are you?'

'I enjoy it, yes.'

'I'd have said fiction was more your style.'

'Why d'you say that?'

'Don't try to take the piss out of me.'

'I don't understand.'

'You will. When was this play on?'

'In the evening.'

'And there was me thinking it was four in the morning. Come on, give me a time.'

'I can't.'

'Now there's a strange thing.'

'Look, it must be in the *Radio Times*. So I can look and see what the time was.'

'Then what's stopping you?'

Lynch stood, crossed to a small, untidy pile of papers and magazines, picked up a magazine and opened it. 'There we are. The play started at nine o'clock.'

'Isn't that just one big coincidence!'

'What?'

'You telling us you were watching at nine o'clock when we were about to ask you what you were doing just after nine. Or maybe it's not a coincidence; maybe you knew the time we were interested in.'

'How could I?'

'Because that was when you were out and about in your car.'

'I don't go driving at night since ... since it happened.'

'Since your friend got himself killed?'

'He was murdered, trying to save the birds.'

'Wouldn't have said birds were his pigeon.'

'I ... I don't understand.'

'You wouldn't. Let's get back to where you were at nine, Wednesday evening.'

'I've just said.'

'You're being so stupid, you're definitely annoying me.'

'I swear I was here, watching the play.'

'And you can tell me all about it because you put it on tape so as you could watch it later and tell us all about it, thinking we were dumb enough to accept that as an alibi. Got that idea out of a book in your library, did you? Out-of-date stock, that's what that was.'

'I swear—'

'You look like a man who oughtn't to swear for fear you'd blush scarlet ... You weren't watching the television; you were in

Brightlee.'

'I don't even know where that is.'

'The Deans live there.'

'Who are they?'

'You should have words with a psychiatrist if you're persecuting someone you don't know.'

'I'm not persecuting anyone.'

'So what do you call heaving a brick through a window with a message on it saying some balls about death earn death? Couldn't find the word "earns" in the paper, couldn't you? Not that that would have made much sense either.'

'What are you talking about?'

'Not being hero material, the moment you'd bunged the brick, you drove off like you thought you were at Silverstone.'

'I didn't drive anywhere, I was here.'

'And I believe in honest politicians! You're really not being smart. Every time you lie to us, you dig yourself a little deeper into the shit.'

'I was here.'

'Going to tell us you lent your car to someone?'

'No.'

'Now there's a sensible decision, since

we'd have asked who your friend was – wouldn't have been able to tell us, would you? So you admit you were driving like the clappers on Wednesday evening away from the Deans' house?'

'I'm not admitting anything.'

'Then you're acting real stupid.'

'I've nothing to admit.'

'Have you asked yourself why we're here?'

'It's because you're continually trying to say I'm persecuting people.'

'We're here because, like I said, someone saw you drive away from the Deans' place with dynamite up the exhaust pipe.'

'I wasn't there, I was here.'

'That someone was so shocked by the speed you were going at, she took the number of your car.'

'When it was dark?'

'How d'you know it was?'

'You've been talking about nine o'clock; it's dark long before then.'

'You're quick; but not all that smart, because you've forgotten there's a light over the number plate so unless someone's blind, they can read it.'

'What did the person tell you?'

'I've said.'

'What number did she say?'

Tudor realized with angry annoyance that he had not earlier checked what the number was. 'Look, we'd like to make things easier for you because you've been through a lot. Intense grief can make a man doolally, doing things he'd normally never do.'

'I haven't been doing anything.'

'You've been sending threatening letters, making threatening phone calls, bunging bricks through windows. Nasty. But when someone's not thinking straight, we don't bruise them, we try to help them. Have you ever been banged up?'

'What are you talking about now?'

'Have you been to prison?'

'Of course I haven't.'

'I thought not, or you'd have been more on the ball. The law has to do its job and catch people who go crook, but it's not heartless. It understands that sometimes a person can kind of not be responsible for what he's done because he's been knocked doolally by what's happened to him. And so the court shows as much sympathy as it's allowed to and provided the crime isn't in the big league, the accused is handed down something like a suspended sentence. No prison. But if he lies and goes on lying, the court knows he's not nearly as disturbed as he's been trying to make out and it loses all sympathy and it's a prison sentence. Nasty places – most especially for blokes like you. In a couple of weeks, you'd grab a ticket to hell with both hands if it got you out of the place.

'But why are we talking about prison? You've shown us you can be sharp, so you're not going to go on lying, knowing the court will lose all sympathy for you and send you off to prison where every day will be forty-eight hours of sheer, bloody misery; you're going to tell us the truth so we can say you've really helped us and the court will understand you didn't know what you were doing to the Deans and there'll be no prison, just a suspended sentence and some community service ... You were in Brightlee on Wednesday evening, weren't you?'

'I was here. I was here,' Lynch said wildly.

Tudor stood. 'Maybe a librarian doesn't have to be all that smart after all. You have the *Guardian*, don't you?'

'Why d'you want to know?'

He didn't answer, went over to the untidy heap of newspapers. Amongst the copies of the *Guardian* was the Wednesday issue. No words had been cut out of it.

Minutes later, Tudor and Lee returned to their car.

'You applied pressure,' Lee said, as he settled in the front passenger seat, 'but I reckon there was a leaky valve.'

Tudor was so annoyed, he stalled the engine as he tried to draw away from the pavement.

Twelve

The provisional report from the forensic laboratory arrived on Tuesday. No finger-prints had been found other than those for which comparison prints had been provided: gloved fingers had been used. The words had been cut from a copy of the *Guardian*; the brick offered no identifying peculiarities.

Tudor swore as he put the report down on his desk.

'The second girlfriend in a week telling you she's pregnant?' Curran asked.

'The lab report on the brick and message thrown through the Deans' window is as much use as a dead donkey.'

'You've still got their bee in your bonnet?'

'Buzzing harder than ever.'

'You want a word of advice?'

About to explain what the other could do

with his advice, Tudor checked the words. Curran might appear to be a somewhat thoughtless, hail-fellow-well-met character, but those who knew him well appreciated that beneath his carelessly boisterous manner was someone more serious. 'I know it probably looks daft, but I can't forget Mrs Dean. It's like seeing a rabbit caught in a snare and trying to pull itself free but only drawing the wire tighter.'

'You've very obviously forgotten all about rule *numero uno* for brothel-keepers and policemen: never allow yourself to become emotionally involved with a customer.'

'And how to avoid that when you see she's being scared silly?'

'Step back.'

'And if you bloody well can't because you know who's scaring her and that if only you could find the proof, you could have him put away and free her from fear?'

'You've given it your best, Sean; and must have come close to putting yourself in the deep end, doing it.'

'The best hasn't been good enough.'

'It happens. But you know what they say: better ninety nine guilty men go free than that one innocent man is jailed.'

'Better for the future victims of the ninety-nine?'

'Ask a bleeding-heart liberal that question.'

Unwin stepped into the room. 'Is this a private mothers' meeting or can anyone join in? ... CCTVs have picked up the image of the flasher who's making wives find their husbands are lacking more than manners. We think we have an identification, so one of you go out and question Dunn. His address will be on file ... That is, of course, if one of you can spare the time.' He left.

'I wonder when's the last time he was even just a little bit happy?' Curran said.

'When was the last time the guv'nor said you were doing a damned good job?'

'Life can be hell, even with women. So do you question this man of noble proportions, or do I?'

'I'm up to my neck in work.'

'And likely to go right under it at any moment, I'd say. Oh well, Joe Soap answers the call of duty with his usual enthusiasm.'

Early Saturday morning, Kay was awoken by Leo's shouting. She threw back the bed-clothes and rushed into the next bedroom to find that he appeared to be sleeping soundly. As the minutes passed, he continued to breathe easily and deeply.

'Is he all right?' Dean mumbled as she returned.

'I think so, but...'

'It was a nightmare.'

'He surely wouldn't shout out like that just because of a nightmare.'

'It seems he would.'

She climbed back into bed and switched off the light. For a while, she mentally catalogued the medical horrors that might suddenly afflict a child and wondered if a sudden shout was a symptom of any one of them.

Dean lay in bed and tried to gauge from the sounds and the quality of the light that escaped the curtains what the weather was like. There was no pattering of rain on the peg tiles of the roof, no whistling draught around the nearest sash window – audible despite the double glazing when the wind was strong and from the south – and the growing daylight had what he called 'an edge to it', which suggested the sky was clear. Conditions should prove to be good for his invitation to Ister – a 'second-day' shoot, which meant outlying fields would be walked for partridges, smaller woods beaten for pheasants, and a couple of the ponds 'shaken' for mallard, widgeon and occasional teal; a day when guns were invited solely in the name of friendship rather than with regard to shooting prowess; a day that might offer a lucky gun the accolade of a right and left at woodcock.

He climbed out of bed, crossed to the nearer window, pulled back the curtains and looked out. His analysis had been correct. The few clouds were high and the top branches of the ancient oak trees at the edge of the five-acre field were moving, but not vigorously. As he turned away from the window, Kay said, 'Have you seen how Leo is?'

Had he not been so certain Leo had merely been suffering from a nightmare, he would have checked on his health before the weather. 'Just about to.'

He made his way along the narrow passage to the first bedroom. Once again, his judgement was correct: Leo was sleeping soundly, breathing normally; his face was not flushed, his forehead not hot.

'How is he?' she asked, as he stepped through the doorway of their bedroom.

'Fighting fit.'

She yawned. 'I didn't sleep very well.'

'Unsurprisingly.'

'I was so worried. I know I fuss too much, my love, but I just can't help that.'

He reached under the bedclothes and held her right hand. 'Try to remember William Weston. "If things were ever as bad as we can imagine them becoming, hell would be a sanctuary." ' He released her hand, and stood. 'Since our son and heir is fast asleep and hopefully will remain so for some time yet, can I tempt you to breakfast in bed?'

'You think I have to be tempted?'

'Then what's the order?'

'Coffee, a couple of slices of toast, and some of that delicious homemade marmalade Muriel gave us. It's on the top shelf of the store cupboard ... But aren't you shooting?'

'At the moment, I am not; later this morning, I hope to be.'

'Preserve me from a pedant ... You'll need a cooked breakfast and I can't lie in bed like a dowager duchess.' She folded back the bedclothes.

He replaced them. 'You are going to have breakfast in bed and a dowager duchess in this day and age is more likely to be helping to polish furniture before the paying crowds enter the stately home.'

'But—'

'But me no buts.'

He went through to the bathroom, dressed, made his way downstairs. The post, on the small bench in the porch, consisted of three letters and a small parcel. He collected them, identified the senders of two of the letters from the handwriting, thought the third might be from a distant cousin, since the postmark was Glasgow, and failed to guess the sender of the parcel because the address had been typed and the postmark was indecipherable.

In the kitchen, he filled the lower half of the coffee machine with water and the container with ground coffee, screwed the two halves together, set them on the stove and switched on a ring. He cut six slices of bread, dropped two into the toaster, having made certain the control was set at 'light' – Kay detested the taste of burned bread – brought the marmalade out of the store cupboard, milk and butter from the refrigerator, and set the tray. The coffee machine hissed. He poured out a cupful, added one spoonful of sugar and a dash of milk, put two pieces of toast in the plated rack that had been a present from her elderly aunt. He put the letter addressed to her on the tray, carried that up to the bedroom and received a kiss and a request to make certain Leo was still asleep.

Back downstairs, he put a non-stick frying pan on the stove after switching on a ring, and dropped two rashers of bacon into the pan before he realized the rind had not been cut off. As he used a pair of kitchen scissors to remove the rind, the toast popped up. He returned the bacon to the frying pan, forgot that was warming, so that he briefly singed his right forefinger, dropped one of the slices of toast and rapped his knuckles as he caught it before it hit the floor. He judged the bacon was cooking too quickly, broke a second egg more enthusiastically than intended on the edge of the frying pan and had to use a spoon to fish out bits of shell, tried to turn off a ring that wasn't on...

He ate. Catering for oneself could have its advantages. The eggs and bacon had been cooked to perfection, the bread toasted with

expert skill; the coffee was nectar. He opened the two letters addressed to him. As he
had judged, the one from Glasgow was from
a distant cousin; the second was from a
couple they had met on a wine-tasting tour
in France – Hugh wrote that he and Frances
would be in their neighbourhood in a
couple of weeks and they hoped he and Kay
would have a meal with them. And, Dean
thought cynically, that their invitation
would be reciprocated by the offer of a bed.

He ate. England's gift to the world of
haute cuisine was breakfast. Did anyone still
serve a full menu? Porridge; bloater, kipper
or haddock; eggs, bacon, kidneys and a
chop; toast and marmalade; fruit.

He went through to the kitchen and poured out a second cup of coffee, added sugar
and milk, returned to the dining room,
sat, picked up the small parcel. A book? He
tried to undo the string – Kay liked to
salvage bits of string; when asked why, she
could offer no rational answer – found the
knots had been drawn too tightly. He
carried the parcel through to the kitchen,
put it down on a working surface, picked up
a steel knife and sliced through the string.
He unwrapped the brown paper. A cigar

box, presumably no longer holding cigars because the seal had been broken and he was known to be a non-smoker. He unclipped the small brass catch and raised the lid. There was a sharp crack of sound a millisecond before a sheet of flame raced up towards the ceiling. Shock held him motionless until pain in his left hand sharpened his mind. He raced into the hall. 'Get down here with Leo,' he shouted. An old house with a wealth of oak beams was a potential fireball...

There were two extinguishers, one upstairs, one downstairs; the latter was at the far end of the hall. As he picked it up, Kay demanded to know what was happening.

'Just get down as fast as you can.' He raced back into the kitchen, withdrew the safety pin of the extinguisher, aimed and depressed the firing lever. Liquid, which immediately turned into foam, speared out. The flames died away as the extinguisher emptied.

He became more aware of the pain in his hand and for the first time rationally understood it had been burned. About to put his hand under the cold tap, he saw a flicker of flame rise above the collapsed foam. He rushed upstairs. Kay was in the doorway of the second bedroom, Leo by her side. 'For God's sake, what's wrong?' she called out.

'Fire.' He picked up the second extinguisher, returned to the kitchen. There was now no flame, but for several minutes he stood, extinguisher in his right hand, thumb on the firing lever. Finally satisfied all danger was past, he put the extinguisher down. He was breathing as rapidly as if he had been running for a distance.

'Where's the fire?' Kay called out from the foot of the stairs.

'It's out.'

'What the hell happened?'

'There was a small parcel in the post. I didn't open it until I'd eaten and then couldn't undo the string so, thank God, I put it on the granite working surface in the kitchen. If it had been on anything flammable, the house might well now be on its way to burning down.'

'How can a parcel catch fire?'

He wanted once more to hide the truth, but accepted that it would be ridiculous to try to do so. 'I think it was some kind of fire-bomb.'

She stared at him for several seconds

before her expression became one of shock and fear. Leo, not understanding, but sensing, her emotions, pressed himself against her, his face hidden in the lower reaches of her dressing gown. 'He ... he sent it?' she said shrilly.

Dean sought to divert her attention before fear overwhelmed her. 'I got slightly burned – is there something I can put on my hand?'

'How badly burned? Show me.' She hurried forward, careless that in doing so she jerked Leo sideways.

Thirteen

'So let's have a run down on the score,' Naylor said.

Unwin, standing in front of the desk, cleared his throat. 'The remains of the box and contents have been sent to Forensic. Virtually all the wrapping paper was burned up, but a very small piece was saved by the foam – not likely to be of any use. There was quite a lot of string.'

'Could Mr Dean give a working description of the parcel?'

'Address was typewritten, postmark illegible. It was a cigar box and there was a broken seal, which might have had on it the name La Corona, but he wouldn't bet a fortune that that's right.'

'Nothing more?'

'No, sir.'

'I think we accept it was a firebomb before

we get Forensic's report.'

'Cigar boxes don't usually burst into flames.'

'Quite.' The detective sergeant, Naylor thought, who had spoken earnestly, not sardonically, had the habit of underlining the obvious. 'Do we accept we know who sent it?'

'Has to be Lynch.'

'Your reason for saying that?'

'The firebomb follows the pattern of written and spoken threats.'

'I understood you doubted Lynch was the source of those threats.'

'The fact is, guv, he seemed a possible from the beginning except for the problem of motive. On the face of things, he didn't have one since Mr Dean hadn't shot Hopkins. But since no one else had one either, I got to thinking that perhaps Lynch believed Mr Dean had shot Hopkins because of the terms in which the inquest was reported in the local paper.'

'I seem to have heard that theory before.'

'Could have been from Tudor. I'd been mulling over the facts, came to a conclusion and asked him what he thought about that. He reckoned it could be right, so I made it

175

obvious I decided it had to be nonsense.'

'A somewhat illogical thing to do, surely?'

'Not really. I did it as a kind of a ... What's it called?'

'Devil's advocate?'

'Could be,' Unwin answered doubtfully. 'You know how it goes. Someone suggests something and you say he's round the twist, so he becomes all the sharper to prove he's right.' He chuckled. 'I knew it was working when he slipped off to have a word with Mr Dean and Lynch without telling me.'

'Then perhaps you see the firebomb as a sign of success for your plan?'

Unwin failed to appreciate the sarcasm. 'In a way, I suppose it is. Got him so sharp, he disturbed Lynch sufficiently to try to do in Mr Dean. Not, of course, that I ever thought Lynch had the bottle to go to such lengths.'

'I'm glad of that.'

'Still, don't they say, "Marry a rich old widow because she's likely to die soon"?'

'I can't say I've heard that recipe for a happy marriage before. You think we'll now learn enough to provide the proof needed to charge Lynch?'

'I do, yes, sir.'

Naylor spoke slowly. 'I wish I could share your optimism when to date he's proved a tad too cunning.' He thought for a moment. 'I'll question him as soon as we get the report from Forensic; optimistically, they'll be able to give us something meaty.'

'I'll go with you...'

'I'll take Tudor. He might have some more absurdly original ideas.' Naylor pulled back the sleeve of his coat and looked at his wrist-watch. 'I'm off home to explain to my wife why yet one more weekend has been scram-bled.'

As Unwin left, Naylor crossed to the old-fashioned stand and lifted off his raincoat. The detective sergeant, he thought, shared certain qualities with a snake.

Dean said, 'Why not go and stay with your sister for a while?'

Kay looked across the sitting room. The shaded bulb above and slightly to the side of him was casting patterns of light and dark-ness, which had the effect of making his face appear more lined, and therefore older, than normal. 'Will you come with me?'

'With the latest project at work beginning to hum, I don't think I can take any time off. But you...'

'I'm not going without you.'

'You and Leo would be safe...'

'It's you, not Leo and me, this madman's trying to kill; he addressed that terrible parcel to you. I'm frightened sick he's going to try to harm you again, and if I'm with you, I can help stop him.'

Or become the classic victim, the person in the middle, he thought grimly.

'What are the police doing?'

'They'll be making inquiries.'

'Judging by what's happened, they'll be more likely wasting their time wondering if you sent the firebomb to yourself.'

'I doubt they believe I'm into burning houses rather than bridges.'

'Why do you so often try to joke about things?'

'It prevents my envisaging too many disasters.'

'Oh, God, Jerome, I'm behaving like a real bitch.'

'You're on edge and I'm making a bull's nest of trying to relieve the tension.'

She finished her drink. 'Would it be terrible to have another one? I know alcohol is a false comforter...'

'But, as any philosopher should know, false comfort is preferable to true discomfort.' He stood, crossed to take the glass from her. 'Same again, but stronger?'

'You'll have me flat out.'

'I was thinking of leaving that pleasure until after supper.'

'Food being more important?'

'Depends which is the hotter.'

'I could throw something at you ... Have I told you how much I love you?'

'Not today.'

'Then do I do so before or after the meal?'

He laughed.

Naylor read the report from Forensic. He had not expected solid evidence, yet was resentfully annoyed that what he received was virtually useless. Fire had destroyed so much of the evidence, little could be stated with confidence. The tiny segment of charred wrapping paper seemed to be of ordinary quality and similar paper was probably available in hundreds of retail outlets – it could offer no meaningful comparisons; tests to bring out anything written had failed. The string, a fairly long piece of which had been saved because it had been put down some way away from the source of the fire, was equally uninformative; the box had been made from echam, a wood commonly used in Cuba in the manufacture of cigar boxes; the six-centimetre length of plumber's piping offered no peculiar characteristics; the ball bearings were of industrial quality, but nothing more about them could be determined. Several pieces of twisted and partially melted metal had almost certainly provided the firing mechanism, but it was not possible to offer more than an inspired guess as to the exact form that had taken. Incompetent design and/or manufacture had resulted in an incendiary device rather than an explosive one. The combustible material had been smokeless powder and the most likely source for that was shotgun cartridges cut open and emptied, although anyone with the authority to load his own cartridges would have had a supply of it.

He put the report down on his desk. Dean had been very lucky. Had the homemade pipe bomb exploded as intended, he would have suffered crippling or fatal injuries. The case had become far more important. Lynch – there was little room for doubt that he was the guilty man – had to be arrested before he made another attempt to murder or, since failure should never be discounted, warned off such an attempt.

He used the internal telephone to call Unwin into his room. A less self-conscious DI would have walked through to the next room, sat on the desk and said what he had to say; but formality reinforced authority.

Unwin entered.

'The report on the bomb is through from Forensic.'

'That's quick.'

'So it should be.' Naylor pushed the two typewritten pages, clipped together, across the desk.

Unwin read, looked up. 'Not much there.'

'Enough to work on,' snapped Naylor, contradicting his previous assessment. 'We'll need a photo of Lynch; do we have one?'

'He's no record, so unless we can find one in the public domain, no.'

'We can't waste time shuffling through newspapers and magazines for a man there's no reason for anyone to want to photograph. Send Allright off in the van and tell him to stay outside Lynch's place until he's snapped the man.'

'He's tied up with the petrol station rob-bery...'

'He can untie himself. As soon as we have copies of a photo, post offices and sub-post offices are to be questioned as to whether any staff can remember Lynch posting a small parcel; shops selling shotgun cart-ridges to be questioned; we can try tracing his purchase of brown paper and string if we have to, but that's lost time from the start ... Do we know what kind of work he does?'

'He's a librarian.'

'Then he has access to computers and the Internet, which probably holds instructions on making a pipe bomb. Does he have a computer at home?'

'I'm not certain.'

'Why not?'

There was a brief silence, which Naylor broke. 'I'll have a word with the Deans later on and with Lynch in the afternoon or evening.'

Kay stepped into the porch and opened the outer door.

'Mrs Dean? My name is Detective Inspec-tor Naylor and my colleague is—'

'We've already met.'

'I imagine your husband is at work?'

'Yes.' Her dark-brown eyes expressed sharp anger. 'Does your coming here mean you're at last treating us seriously?'

'I can assure you—'

'And I can assure you, I've been frightened sick because until my husband's been nearly burned to death, the police have thought we were just being silly.'

'That is not correct.'

'You would try to claim that, now you've been proved so terribly wrong.'

'I can understand your feelings, Mrs Dean, which is why I should very much like to explain one or two things to you.' When there was reason, Naylor could project caring sympathy. 'May we come in?'

She stepped back and they entered the hall.

'You've a very charming house,' Naylor said, as he stared up at the sloping ceiling.

She ignored his remark, led the way into the sitting room. 'Would you like to sit?' Her tone suggested it was only politeness that made her willing to offer even basic hospitality.

Once settled, Naylor said, 'I'm here in a

large part because I decided we owed it to you to explain why we have acted as we have. What I would ask you to remember is that at all times we are constrained by the need to remain within the boundaries the law sets, whatever the circumstances, however much easier it would make our task if we were to move outside them. So while it has, I am certain, been very difficult for you to appreciate this, we have been doing our very best to identify the person responsible for the threats to your husband.'

'I understood you had already done so,' she said sharply.

'Had done what, Mrs Dean?'

'Identified him.'

'Why should you think that?'

'You know who he is, but can't arrest him.'

'If we had identified someone and could be certain of the identification, I can assure you we would have arrested him; the point is, there cannot be certainty until there is proof.'

'Small wonder crime is flourishing.'

'As I've tried to explain—'

'Your explanation alters nothing. My husband has been repeatedly threatened by a madman and three days ago was nearly

184

burned to death by that God-awful bomb. Yet you come here to try to explain why you know who sent it, but can't arrest him.'

'When we cannot be certain who is guilty.'

'Because you can't legally prove he is? My husband's life is so much less important than the rules?'

'There have to be rules to protect the—'

She interrupted him. 'To protect the guilty. The innocent, of course, have no protection.'

'I'm sure you don't really think that.'

'When I need to find out what I'm thinking, I won't ask a policeman who'll say he can only answer me when he can prove my thoughts.'

'I'm sorry you should feel like that, Mrs Dean.'

'How do you expect me to feel in the circumstances?'

'I'm hoping,' Naylor finally said, 'that you'll be able to help us find the necessary proof.'

'How?'

'By telling us all you can about what's happened.'

'Both my husband and I have already done so.'

'You have been very helpful – very helpful indeed. But it is true that if someone is asked to repeat his evidence, quite often he provides a small fact that he had forgotten before, a fact seemingly of no significance to him, yet of great importance to us.'

During the next twenty minutes, Naylor learned nothing fresh of any significance. He thanked her for her understanding help and he and Tudor left.

As he drove out on to the road, he said sharply, 'Who told her about Lynch?'

'Did anyone?' Tudor answered.

'You heard her say she understood that we knew the target, but couldn't find the proof to arrest him. You let your tongue hang loose when you were here before.'

'Certainly not, sir.'

'No one else could have told her.'

'With respect, sir, as you've been explaining to her, unless there's the proof no one else could have given her the facts...'

'Try to get smart with me and I'll have you back in uniform before nightfall.'

Clearly, Tudor thought, guilty DCs were not protected by the same rules of evidence as guilty civilians.

Fourteen

Street lights were on as Naylor turned into Well Road. 'What's the number?'

'Two,' Tudor replied.

They continued along the road until, nearly at the end, there was a parking space. Naylor backed in, but not tightly enough; he drew out, tried again; at the third attempt, he succeeded in parking the car nearly two feet away from the pavement. 'This car has a poor lock.'

And an even poorer driver, Tudor thought.

'You start the questioning and take it nice and quietly. I'll come in when I think that's necessary.'

'Sir.' The old hard/soft technique of interrogation. Occasionally, it did work.

Lynch opened the front door of number 2 and, in the light that came from the hall, recognized Tudor.

'Evening, Mr Lynch,' Tudor said cheerfully. 'This is Detective Inspector Naylor.'

Lynch looked quickly at Naylor, then away.

'We'd like a word.'

'Why?'

'We think you may be able to help us.'

'I don't know nothing. I never sent any messages; I never threw no brick.'

'That's not why we're here.'

'What then?'

'We'll explain, but it'll be a lot more comfortable inside. Don't mind us coming in, do you?' Tudor said, as he stepped into the hall, closely followed by Naylor.

The front room had been tidied, but the black ribbon was still covering part of the photograph of Hopkins, and a plate, knife and fork were on the coffee table. The television was on; Tudor used the remote control to switch it off.

'I'm watching...' Lynch began weakly.

'That programme isn't worth the effort.'

'If I want to watch in me own house...'

'So you can, once we've had our chat.'

'I can't help when I don't know nothing.'

'Then we'll very soon be able to leave you in peace.'

Tudor and Naylor sat; finally, Lynch did the same.

'Just for the record,' Tudor said, 'you're a librarian – right?'

'What's it matter?'

'Like I said, just for the record.'

'But I don't understand...'

'We're not asking you to understand,' Naylor said sharply.

Lynch moved uneasily.

'You're a librarian?' Tudor said for the second time.

After a long pause, Lynch answered. 'Yes.'

'Where do you work?'

'At the local public library.'

'Then you'll know where to look to find out about almost anything?'

'I suppose.'

'Like how to make a pipe bomb?' Naylor said sharply.

'There won't be books telling anything like that.'

'How can you know if you haven't searched?'

'I ... I just do.'

'Do you have a computer at home?' Tudor asked.

'No.'

'But there's one in the library?'

'Yes.'

'So you used that to find out how to make the pipe bomb,' Naylor said, stating a fact, not asking a question.

'What are you on about?'

Tudor waited until it became clear Naylor intended to remain silent for the moment. 'Do you smoke cigars?'

'I don't smoke.'

'Did Hopkins use them?'

'I ... I can't remember.'

'Then he did, but you'd rather we didn't know,' Naylor said.

Lynch, not conscious of doing so, gripped the arm of the settee.

'I wonder why you're so reluctant to tell us?'

'I just can't remember,' he said weakly.

'And pigs shit corn flakes. You're forgetting because you packed the pipe bomb into the cigar box you sent to Mr Dean.'

'I've never sent him anything.'

'I haven't met a more useless liar since a tea-leaf swore he hadn't nicked a half bottle of whisky when it was sticking out of his pocket. You sent him a threatening letter through the post and another with the help of a brick ... Do you shoot?'

Lynch had trouble in adjusting his mind to the change of subject. 'No.'

'Why not?'

'It's cruel.'

'I like that,' Naylor said. He turned to Tudor. 'Don't you just like that?'

'A real classic.'

He spoke to Lynch again. 'You don't like shooting because it's cruel to birds, but in your book, trying to murder someone is good, clean fun.'

'I haven't tried to murder anyone.'

'Not anyone – someone. Mr Dean ... Have you bought any shotgun cartridges recently?'

'I've never bought any.'

'You're hoping we won't identify the shop that sold you a couple of boxes? I'll give you this, you're a real optimist. Isn't that right, he's a real optimist?'

'Soon be thinking we'll believe him.' He was becoming, Tudor decided, the Greek chorus.

'I wonder...' Naylor stopped.

Lynch's face expressed his growing tension.

'I wonder if you really can be so dim as to

hope we'll believe you or whether you've some ulterior motive for wanting us to think you're a useless liar?'

'I'm telling the truth.' Lynch's voice was shrill.

'Then you're completely innocent of anything and to help prove that, you're not going to object to us searching your house.'

'Why d'you want to do that?'

'To confirm what you've told us.'

'You're not going to.'

'Not going to be able to prove your innocence?'

'Not going to search.'

'You're making us very curious. Isn't he making us very curious?' Naylor asked Tudor.

'Just like Alice, guv,' Tudor dutifully replied.

Naylor spoke to Lynch again. 'Would you like to know why you're making us so curious?'

There was no reply.

'When you don't want us to have a look around to confirm your innocence, we get to wondering what you're hiding and don't want us to see. From the look of you, a rubber doll gives you lots of fun. But rubber

192

dolls are just a joke compared to some of the things we come across. So it's something much more incriminating. Empty cartridge cases, more of your partner's cigar boxes, instructions for making a pipe bomb that you called down from the Internet at the library? So save us time and tell us which it is. Or maybe it's all of them, plus some videos that could have you up in court.'

'There's nothing here.'

'Then you can't have a reason for refusing us.'

'You ain't doing it without a search warrant.'

'You reckon that could save you? No one's ever going to accuse you of having good street cred. We can be back here with a warrant before you've had time to change your pants. And when we come back, we'll be so pissed off at you wasting our time, we'll turn everything inside out and run you in on a dozen charges.'

'The detective inspector's talking right,' Tudor said quietly. 'If you've nothing to hide, then it makes sense to let us have a look around so we convince ourselves you've been telling the truth right along and we're a shower ever to have disbelieved you.'

'You don't do anything without a warrant.'

'You couldn't lie your way out of a fairy ring,' Naylor said. 'You sent the letter, made the phone call, heaved the brick through the window, posted the pipe bomb.'

Lynch stared fixedly at the floor in front of his shoes.

'You're not only a bloody hopeless liar, you're also so thick you still don't understand Mr Dean did not fire the shot that killed your partner.'

Lynch looked up. 'Who did, then?'

'Not for you to know.'

'Then it was him.'

'It was not and you're a long way down the road to doing time for being stupid. So get smart and make things easier for everyone. A good word from the investigating officer can count heavy with the bench. But it's just as simple to slip in a few words that make the bench think they've got Jack the Ripper in the dock.'

'You ain't doing nothing without a warrant.'

Tudor took up the questioning. 'Have you got a typewriter?'

'Why d'you want to know?'

'It's easily explained after you've said if

194

you've got one.'

'Yes,' Lynch finally answered.

'Where is it?'

'Upstairs.'

'We'll go and have a look at it.'

'You ain't going anywhere.'

'Then you'll have to bring it down here.'

'Why?'

'So as I can type out Mr Dean's name and address and that can be compared with the typing on the brown paper that was wrapped around the cigar box in which the pipe bomb was. The experts can always say if something was typed out on a certain typewriter.'

'I ... I've just remembered.'

'What?'

'I lent it to a friend.'

'Balls!' Naylor said.

'That's straight.'

'As straight as a cat's cradle. What friend?'

'Mike.'

'And the rest.'

'Mike Penfold.'

'Address?'

'Little Pitchley, Cannonbridge.'

Tudor wrote down the name and address. When Naylor said nothing, he continued the questioning. 'You know how the threatening messages to Mr Dean were constructed, of course.'

'No, I don't.'

'With words cut out of a newspaper. I told you that before.'

'I forgot.'

'You must have trouble remembering whether it's night or day. What newspaper provided the words that were cut out?'

'How would I know?'

'Something more you've forgotten? They came out of the *Guardian*. You take that paper.'

'It's just a coincidence.'

'You're amassing so many coincidences, you ought to be in the *Guinness Book of Records*. In the first message, because you couldn't find the word "bastard", you had to write it out by hand in capitals. You used capitals because you thought that made it more difficult to compare handwriting. Was that something you picked up from a book in the library?'

Lynch did not answer.

'Difficult does not mean impossible. Perhaps the book you consulted was out of date. Now, it's been confirmed that capitals can be sufficiently individualistic to offer a definite identification. Did you write the word "bastard" in the message Mr Dean received?'

'No.'

'Then why did you refuse to write out the word for me when I spoke to you before?'

'I didn't send the letter so there was no point.'

'No point in proving your innocence?'

'I don't like being accused of something I ain't done.'

'Write it out for us now and we'll be able to confirm you didn't send that message; then, we won't need to accuse you of anything again.'

'I won't.'

Naylor stood. 'It's going to be a pleasure to nail you for the lying bastard you are,' he said, before he left the room.

Four minutes later, within yards of having drawn out into the road, they missed an oncoming car by inches. Naylor expressed his opinion of the other driver.

'Do we go for a search warrant?' Tudor asked, after his nerves had settled.

'And have the magistrate give us hell for wasting his precious time with evidence that wouldn't convict Torquemada of simple assault?'

Naylor, Tudor judged, was clearly now just as convinced as he that Lynch was their target and the refusal to allow them to search the house or provide a specimen of writing had been motivated by fear, not an overdeveloped sense of civil liberty. But without the necessary evidence to persuade a magistrate, they were powerless to pursue their certainties.

Fifteen

Naylor would usually listen to other people's opinions and advice, but seldom accepted the validity of the one or the advisability of the other; to do either might suggest uncertainty on his part. He was about to go down to the conference room when a PC knocked on the door, entered and handed him a faxed report from Forensic. He read it through and put it in a folder, which he took with him when he left the room.

As he entered the conference room, Unwin and Tudor stood, an old-fashioned courtesy he did not discourage. He sat at the near end of the long, rectangular table. 'Forensic have finally sent their confirmatory report on the message wrapped around the brick that was thrown through the Deans' window. Nothing new. Similar paper to the last note, obtainable in a thousand

and one outlets; no prints, only impressions made by gloved fingers, nothing offering DNA; the four rubber bands are of a type made in their millions, and the brick is standard London, impossible to trace.'

'To be expected,' Unwin said gloomily.

'Expect nothing and you find nothing.'

'When he's proved himself so smart...'

'Am I wasting my time to expect someone in CID to be that little bit smarter?' Naylor opened the folder, brought out a sheet of paper and briefly read. 'Any joy on the sale of cartridges?' he asked, as he replaced it.

'The staff in every shop with the necessary licence have been questioned and shown the photograph of Lynch, but no joy,' Unwin answered.

'Post offices?'

'Always the same answer: too many customers to remember an individual unless there's reason, like an argument.'

'Cigars?'

'No local shop stocks La Corona cigars.'

'Dean admits he may be mistaking the name.'

'Lynch's photo produced another negative result. And if it was Hopkins who bought them...'

'Quite. Typewriter?'

'Penfold agrees Lynch lent him a typewriter, but says he accidentally dropped it from a height, which wrecked it. So he bought Lynch a new one and pitched the remains of the old one.'

'He expects us to believe that nonsense?'

'Unless we can prove he's lying, he's laughing.'

'Has he got form that might help wipe the smile off his face?'

Unwin hesitated.

'You haven't checked?'

'There's been so much...'

'Find out. Has anyone shown sufficient initiative to have the computer at the library searched?'

'They've got two. An expert has worked on them and says there's nothing been recorded on the making of a pipe bomb.'

'Then we're getting nowhere fast.'

'Seems that way, sir. Looks like the case will have to return to the back burner.'

'Sir,' said Tudor, speaking for the first time, 'instead of easing off, as the sarge is suggesting, we need to pursue the sale of legitimate cartridges, extend the search area, find out if anyone's shifting 'em on the side, question people who—'

'And tie up hands who are needed on other cases?'

'More important ones?'

'It's a case that can't offer any movement. Whereas we've something solid to work on in the wages snatch at Frailbridge which has left two men in hospital, one of 'em given only a fifty-fifty chance of coming through with an undamaged brain.'

'But Mrs Dean is—'

'Forget her,' snapped Unwin.

'She's scared silly and you can't blame her. If we don't—'

'The guv'nor decides priorities, not you.'

Naylor said, 'The Deans have suffered no further persecution since we questioned Lynch. That gives us good reason to think we may have frightened him off.'

'When it must have become obvious we suspected him, but didn't have any hard evidence against him? He's waiting for things to cool and then he'll have another go at murdering Mr Dean.'

'You are forgetting I assured Lynch that Mr Dean did not fire the fatal shot.'

'He'd been told that before.'

'But not by me.'

'That's going to make a difference?'

'I will overlook the inference,' Naylor said, meaning he would remember it.

'It's just I can't stop thinking how scared Mrs Dean is, sir.'

'It is unfortunate you have clearly allowed yourself to become emotionally involved,' Naylor said sharply.

'A bit difficult not to, if one's any imagination.'

'And a hindrance to a career if one has too much ... That's all.'

As Tudor left the room, he heard Naylor say, 'Clearly, a dipping mob has started working Redford, so we're going to have to warn shop owners, get out on the streets and disrupt their operation...' Tudor closed the door and the DI was no longer audible.

He went down a floor to the CID general room, crossed to his desk, sat down. He stared unseeingly at the two forms he should have filled in the previous day. Naylor could always justify his decision that the Dean case must be moved to the back burner. There was not the evidence to arrest Lynch; it had to be far from certain that further investigation, costing many man-hours of work, would turn up the necessary further evidence; the attempt to murder Dean had failed and that might convince him to forgo any further attempt to gain vengeance; priorities were constantly having to be made that must disadvantage someone. Yet all the time Lynch was not under arrest he was free to make a mockery of Naylor's decision ... Too much imagination was more than a hindrance to a career; it was a threat.

Time might not have closed memory's eyes, but as the days and weeks passed and there were no more threats or bombs, Kay ceased to tense every time the phone rang, fear the mail, or suffer sudden panics that Leo was in danger and have to rush and find him and make certain he was all right.

She had, even before Leo had been born, always made certain Christmas would be a Dickensian Christmas. There was already a seven-foot tree in the hall, festooned with coloured lights that worked most of the time, and every room had traditional decorations, which included paper chains (only found with great difficulty). A side of smoked salmon, a whole Stilton, a fifteen-pound turkey, sausage stuffing and a York ham had been ordered; the remaining independent greengrocer in town had promised top-quality sprouts. The Christmas pudding had been made in the spring and throughout the rest of the year frequent additions of brandy guaranteed it did not dry out; mincemeat tarts would be made in the next few days; crackers were in the dining-room sideboard and when they were pulled, paper hats would be worn despite her husband's objection to the ritual humiliation. Her sister and husband would arrive on Christmas Eve – Norris occasionally sucked his lips with a plopping noise that intrigued Leo. The cellar – racks in the bottom of the china cupboard – was well stocked with champagne, burgundy, gin, whisky, cognac and two bottles of ancient Quinta da Cavadinha.

'I hope everything's in hand,' she said, as they ate breakfast.

'Good,' Dean answered, as he read an article in *The Times* detailing expenses that could be claimed by members of the European parliament – never in the field of human profligacy had so much been paid to so many for so little.

'The butcher's promised to deliver the tripe in time for Christmas lunch.'

'Good.'

She said sharply, 'You're not listening to a word I say.'

He looked up. 'On the contrary, to every word.'

'What did I tell you the butcher was doing?'

'Delivering the dressed turkey on Christmas Eve together with the sausage stuffing.'

'I can't think why I bother to talk to you.'

'To profit from the pearls of wisdom that continually fall from my lips.'

'I was so certain you weren't listening, I said the butcher would be delivering tripe.'

'He's gone into politics?'

'I don't know whether to throw something at you or kiss you.'

'Solve the problem by doing both things at once and throw me a kiss.'

'What's made you so bumptious?'

'Did I forget to tell you?'

'Tell me what?'

'Tom Evans stunned us all yesterday evening by announcing his retirement at the end of the year.'

'I thought you reckoned he was determined to stay on until they carried him out of the office in a coffin.'

'I did.'

'Where's that going to leave you?'

'Next door to Joe, and since he's said he'll retire at sixty and go out to New Zealand to be with his daughter, I should be senior partner this time next year.'

'Will that mean an increase in what you have to do?'

'A senior partner's task is making certain the junior partners are doing all the work. Haven't I said that before?'

'Many times. But knowing you, you'll work twice as hard to make certain everything is done exactly. I'm worried you'll do far too much.'

'I've learned to pace myself in my old age ... Who's that?'

'What's the matter?'

'A car's just driven in.'

It was the postman. When Dean met him in the porch, he apologized for the late delivery, due to the volume of post, and handed over a dozen letters and two parcels.

Dean returned to the dining room, put the mail on the table by Kay's side, sat, and buttered another piece of toast.

She opened the envelopes, commenting on messages in the Christmas cards as she did so. 'The Tennants are in Nice.'

'They must have read that it's become chic again to be seen there.'

'They're not such slaves to fashion as you seem to think.'

'I doubt they've ever made a choice on their own judgement.'

'The Morleys have moved, which means I probably should send another card to their new address ... Vivien Yates died back in the summer.'

'The rest of the family had their Christmas present early.'

'That's being nasty.'

'The old girl made their life miserable.'

'It's one of the disadvantages of age.'

'So we'll make Leo's life hell?'

'We'll try not to, but we're bound to become a nuisance ... Jane's getting a divorce.'

'Which Jane?'

'Jane Kennedy.'

'But she only married a couple of years ago.'

'Six years.' She put down the last of the envelopes and picked up the larger of the two parcels. 'It's from Virginia.'

'Has anyone ever been more inappropriately named?'

'You're presuming an origin for the name that I don't believe is fact.'

'In her case, it certainly wasn't, from an early age. What's she sent this time?'

'I've no idea.'

'A lacuna easily rectified.'

'Nothing will be opened until after break-fast on Christmas Day.'

'The ultimate traditionalist!'

'And proud of it.'

'I'll wager she's sent another tablecloth embroidered by someone who's colour-blind.'

'It's the thought that counts.'

'My thought is, each year she's given table linen and keeps it until the following Christ-mas when she sends it on to us.'

'You're becoming horribly uncharitable.' She put the parcel to one side, picked up the other. 'It's for Leo.'

'From your sister?'

'She'll be bringing the presents with her. It was posted in Spain, so it must be from Harry and Jane.'

'They're in Spain?'

'I did tell you, but of course you weren't listening. Harry's arthritis has been worse than usual and they decided to stay somewhere near Marbella in the hope the better weather would do it some good.'

'Jane's proved an unusually conscientious godmother – hasn't missed a Christmas.'

'Or a birthday. And she gave Leo that lovely gilded christening cup.'

'The right kind of godmother to have.'

'That's a commercial outlook.'

'It's a commercial world.'

'Put both parcels up in our bedroom cup-board, will you? I don't think Leo has yet learned to go hunting.'

The office Christmas luncheon was held at the George Hotel, in the banqueting hall – a medium-sized room decorated with con-siderable tastelessness. The meal was stock suburban, but there was sufficient to drink to ensure Thomas Evans's farewell speech was well received. The party continued until the staff, being British, decided it was time for guests to eff off.

Dean left the hotel with two associates and was about to return with them to the office when he remembered he'd promised to pick up a pair of earrings Kay had ordered for her sister. He made his way along the gently sloping High Street and was about to turn into a side street when a voice halted him.

'Afternoon, Mr Dean.'

He turned to face Tudor, and returned the greeting.

'I hope everything's all right?'

'Certainly peaceful. No more threats or pipe bombs.'

'Glad to hear it.'

'Frankly, what would make me really glad to hear is that the bastard had been locked up.'

'I can't say this officially, but I don't think you have to worry any longer. He's left the country, which we read as meaning he's been scared off.'

'You're finally admitting you know who he is?'

'I'll just say, we have a good idea. As so often, our trouble...' He was pushed aside by a hurrying man who did not pause to apologize. 'Our trouble has been,' he continued, when once more within earshot, 'we haven't had the proof to act decisively.'

'But you really do reckon we don't have to worry any more?'

'That's right.'

'Then you've given me the best possible news to pass on to my wife.'

'I'm glad of that, Mr Dean.'

They said goodbye. Dean continued to the jeweller's at the end of the road and was surprised at the cost of the earrings.

'Here you are.' Dean brought the small, velvet-lined box out of his coat pocket.

'You remembered!' Kay said.

'Why the surprise?' he asked, as he hung up his overcoat.

'I imagined that, by the end of the luncheon party, you'd have trouble knowing your way.'

'It was not a Bacchanalian orgy.'

'But you must have had a fair amount to drink, since you're sounding pompous.'

'Thank you for those few kind words.'

She laughed, leaned forward to kiss him on the cheek.

They went into the sitting room and sat on either side of the fireplace, in which several logs were burning in the fire-basket. 'En route to the jeweller's, I met Tudor.'

'Who?'

'Detective Constable Tudor; the young chap who always seemed to be more sympathetic and understanding than the others.'

Lines suddenly appeared in her face and

when she spoke, her voice was strained: 'Did he have anything to say?'

'He gave us a Christmas present. We don't have to worry any more. The man responsible for all that's happened has been scared off by the police.'

'If they're finally accepting they do know who it is, why in the hell haven't they arrested him?'

He explained yet again why the police were unable to act, but it was obvious she was determined not to understand. He was not surprised.

Sixteen

The phone rang when Kay and her sister were out, helping to give a Christmas dinner to the elderly of the parish. Dean stood. 'Tell me the rest when I get back.' Not that Norris needed prompting; his brother-in-law (sister-in law's husband, when he was feeling pedantic) never cut a long story short.

In the hall, he picked up the receiver.

'Harry here, Jerome.'

'How are things and why aren't you in Spain?'

'You think the Spaniards haven't discovered telephones?'

He laughed. 'Stupidly, I just assumed you wouldn't be phoning from there.'

'Jane said I must and when The Great One speaks, I obey.'

'So how's the Med?'

'Blue skies every day, the sun hot enough for swimming, and the evenings perfect for sitting out and enjoying a few *copas* of the local brew. What's the weather like with you?'

'No doubt you hope it's been raining all day and there's an icy wind from the north.'

'Now why should I be hoping that?'

'In order to enjoy your good fortune even more.'

'Jane's right. You are a sarky sod! ... I'm ringing to express her apologies.'

'What's she been up to?'

'In the rush of coming out here, she forgot Leo's Christmas present, which is in a cupboard, waiting to be wrapped up. So she wants you to buy him something and say it's from her and she'll keep what she has for his birthday. And you're expressly commanded to get something he'll like and not what you think he ought to like.'

Five minutes later, after a general conversation and a disquisition on the incapacitating effects of arthritis, Dean replaced the receiver and returned to the sitting room.

'As I was telling you, this Irishman...'

One could always rely on Norris to be amusingly politically incorrect. Yet Dean's attention was not on what was being said. Something was wrong, but he could not identify what. Had he remembered to increase the temperature at which the boiler was set to make certain there was sufficient hot water for everyone? He had. Had Kay asked him to do something while she was at the village hall? No. Was he supposed to have bought something from the local store? If so, he couldn't remember what that was and in any case it was now far too late to do anything about it.

He tried to clear his thoughts. 'How's your glass?'

'The bottom's shining.'

'Then I'm a poor host.' He stood, picked up the bottle of Veuve Clicquot encased in a keep-cool pack, refilled both their glasses and sat down.

'Did I tell you about the chap I met the other day who'd spent a fortnight in Paris on expenses?' Norris asked.

'No.'

'Someone in the Paris office suggested a show. He thought it would be something like the Lido. It did start off typical ooh-la-la, but then the ladies...'

Dean's mind wandered again, despite the

erotic descriptions. Had he left something undone at work? Should he have ... His mind suddenly advanced a gear and he became convinced the cause of his worry stemmed from the recent phone call. Yet what had Harry said to cause him any concern? He'd been asked to buy a present for Leo because Jane had forgotten to send the one she had bought ... But she had sent a parcel, which had arrived the previous Friday. It was unlike Jane to forget – Harry complained that she'd a memory like a computer, especially when to his disadvantage...

The possibility came to mind with such emotional force, it was as if the air had suddenly been knocked out of his lungs. He stood.

'Something wrong?' Norris asked.

He did not answer, crossed to the door-way, went into the hall and over to the phone. He picked up the receiver, replaced it. Was he making a fool of himself, letting his imagination run riot? Tudor had told him there was no longer any cause for fear. But he might be wrong. And Kay had said the parcel for Leo must be from Jane because it had been posted in Spain, which meant she had not identified Jane as the sender from the handwriting – had not recognized the handwriting. Better to make a fool of himself than later tragically learn his fears had been justified.

He dialled 999, said he wanted to speak to Detective Constable Tudor. He was politely – but with a hint of impatience – informed he should ring local Divisional HQ. He found his hands were shaking as he thumbed through the directory for the number.

'Redford police station.'

'I want to speak to Detective Constable Tudor.'

'Your name?'

'Dean.'

'One moment, please, Mr Dean.'

One moment became three, which seemed like fifteen; fear, especially when of something undetermined, could destroy time's march even more thoroughly than Einstein.

'I'm sorry, Mr Dean, DC Tudor is not in the station.'

'How do I get hold of him?'

'If you ring tomorrow morning...'

'I have to speak to him now.'

'I'm afraid...'

'What's his home telephone number?'

'I am not allowed to give that.'

'For God's sake, man, this is urgent.'

'Perhaps you should speak to another member of CID.'

He could easily recall the lack of sympathy and understanding of the other detectives he had met. 'Ring Tudor and ask him to get in touch with me immediately. Tell him it may be a matter of life and death.'

There was a pause, then the speaker said, 'I'll do what I can, Mr Dean.'

If he could be bothered, if he didn't decide the call had been from a weirdo, if something else didn't turn up to make him forget, Tudor thought as he replaced the receiver. He turned and saw Norris was standing in the doorway of the sitting room.

'I couldn't help hearing...' Norris stopped, embarrassed because it might seem he had been eavesdropping. 'When you got up so suddenly, looking as if you'd seen a ghost, I thought you'd been taken ill and so I came out to see if there was anything I could do...' He stopped.

Dean accepted he should satisfy the other's curiosity. He returned into the sitting room, sat, and explained the circumstances.

'You think it's another pipe bomb?'

'I hope it isn't. I hope I'm thinking like a bloody fool.' He stared at the fire, cursing the fact that his actions must cause Kay to relive her terror even if his fears proved to be unfounded.

The phone rang. He hurried out of the room.

'The station has just been on to me, Mr Dean, and told me you'd some sort of trouble?' Tudor said.

Dean answered, ironically suffering the growing conviction he was proving himself a fool.

'Does this parcel look anything like the last one?'

'It's much larger and only half as thick.'

'Does the inside feel solid?'

'I don't remember what it's like.'

'Your wife definitely did not recognize the writing?'

It was not the time to admit it was supposition that she had not. 'She didn't, no.'

'But the name and address are hand-written in cursive script.'

Such was his mental confusion, he had to think what was meant. 'Yes.'

'Then on the face of things, it does seem unlikely it was sent by chummy, because he's well aware that handwriting offers comparison tests, which is why he's always used capitals. But he's probably smart enough to realize you'll be very wary of anything addressed in capitals and so it would pay to get someone else to do the writing.'

'But am I talking nonsense?'

'With what's happened, I'd say you're being sensibly cautious. Where's the parcel now?'

'In the cupboard in our bedroom.'

'I'll get the bomb squad along, but that may take a while. I imagine you've got fresh fire extinguishers or had the others recharged?'

'Yes.'

'Have them handy and keep everyone well away from the bedroom. Do you have smoke alarms?'

'In the hall and landing.'

'If you can, move one into your bedroom. And I think those are about the only immediate precautions I can suggest you take. Let's hope it is a false alarm.'

'You what?' Naylor shouted over the phone.

'I've called in the bomb squad...' Tudor began.

'Without reference to me?'

'I phoned you at home, sir, but you weren't there.'

'I'm out for half an hour and that's time enough for you to make a donkey's arse of everything because you reckon you've a mission in life.'

'It seemed necessary to move very quickly, remembering the pipe bomb.'

'You're saying it's a ton of Semtex just because the wife didn't recognize the hand-writing and it was posted in Italy?'

'Spain.'

'What's it matter if it was the bloody Sahara?'

'Our information is that Lynch has gone to Majorca on a holiday that was booked before Hopkins was killed.'

'Have you never heard of coincidences? What the hell do you think the top brass is going to say when they learn the bomb squad was called out because a DC in my division suffers from hallucinations?'

'The circumstances being what they—'

'The circumstances being what they are, you're going to be knocking on the counter of the nearest unemployment office.' Naylor cut the connexion.

Tudor replaced the receiver. If he had placed his career on the line, so be it. A man could only do what he considered to be right at the time ... But might he have been too hasty in acting on someone else's assessment, someone who was making an explosion out of a damp squib?

Kay and Muriel arrived home soon after nine. As they were helped out of their coats in the hall, they said the evening had been an undoubted success, the old dears had enjoyed the meal – even Mrs Herbert, who was having such trouble with her teeth. The vicar had thanked them for their help and, being a man of optimism, had expressed the certainty he would see them and their husbands in church on Thursday. Mrs Young had almost caused a row, thanks to her unbridled tongue, but Molly, the vicar's wife...

'There's something to tell you,' Dean said.

'You wouldn't like to wait until I've finished speaking?' Kay asked sweetly.

'It's important.'

'Come along,' Norris said to Muriel.

'Where to?'

'Our bedroom.'

223

'What on earth for?'

'Not what you're probably thinking.'

'They say there's always a first time.' Looking puzzled, she followed him up the stairs.

'Has something happened to Leo?' Kay said.

'He's sleeping soundly.'

'But something's wrong, isn't it?'

'Let's go in.' He held open the sitting-room door.

She stared at him for several seconds before she finally went through the doorway, to come to a halt near the central beam. 'What's the matter?'

He explained.

'Oh, Christ! It was supposed to be all over.' Her voice shook. 'You told me he'd been scared off and we didn't have to worry any more.'

'I may be wrong about the parcel.'

'Where's Leo?'

'I said, in bed, fast asleep.'

'Why didn't you get him up? Don't you care he could be in terrible danger?'

'That's not fair.'

'I thought you loved your son, but you don't give a damn about him.'

'You're becoming hysterical.'

'That's so astonishing? After living for weeks knowing someone wants to kill you, I come home and find Leo's sleeping in the room next to a bomb; am I supposed to stiffen my upper lip and just say what a bore it all is? I'm taking him to Pat's.' She turned and hurried over to the door.

'I'll bring him down.'

'You're sure that won't be too much trouble?' she asked with bitter, wild animosity.

The bomb squad consisted of four men, a sergeant and three PCs. Their Transit van contained the equipment necessary to make a preliminary investigation where it was judged safe (in bomb-disposal terms) to carry this out; if it was decided the situation was potentially too dangerous, Big Bertha – an electrical robot – was called for.

The sergeant questioned Dean at length and considered the answers he had been given; since the parcel would have suffered vigorous handling in transit and Dean had carried it upstairs to put it into the cupboard, the odds had to be against any form of trembler fuse. He donned a heavy suit padded with Kevlar, a helmet with bulletproof glass, gloves and boots. He asked Dean to show him the parcel, then ordered him out of the house. Minutes later, the parcel held in front of himself, he crossed to the centre of the lawn and put it down in the beams of three spotlights on tripods.

A sensitive metal detector gave a nil reading. The small, mobile X-ray unit, powered with a lead plugged into the house's circuit, recorded nothing to alarm. The sergeant used a knife to slice through the wrapping paper to reveal a red-and-gold box that contained chocolates in the shapes of favoured cartoon characters.

When Dean rang Pat's house and told Kay what had happened and that she could return home, he had expected relief, not the anger with which his news was received.

Seventeen

As he wrapped up the small presents in crêpe paper and passed them to Kay, Dean was grateful Christmas was working its magic. Her anger of the previous night, born of fear and, ironically, relief, had vanished and she was now her usual, bubbly self, indulging in her love of tradition by filling stockings not only for Leo, but also for her sister and brother-in-law.

He picked up a book, opened it, and began to read.

'Come on, love, or we'll not get to bed before it's time to get up.'

'I must remember to ask Piers if I can borrow this when he's finished it.'

'I don't know if it's quite his style, but the reviews were good and it's set in Queensland. He's always said he wants to live there when he retires.'

'Do you know why?'

227

'It's been the dream to see him through the bitchiness of office life. He imagines himself fishing for barries and having barbies and tinnies on the back lawn.'

'If I knew what you're talking about, I might follow the dream.'

'Stop being so English.'

'Where have you been learning the vocabulary? From Piers? If he's hoping the local lingo will enable him to escape detection as a Pom, he's very optimistic.'

The phone on the small table at the side of the bed rang.

'Who on earth is calling at this hour?' she asked rhetorically. 'Hurry up and answer it before it wakes people up.'

He stood, crossed to the bed, sat as he lifted the receiver.

'Mr Dean?'

'Speaking.'

'Have a jolly Christmas.' There was a laugh, then the connexion was cut.

'Who was it?' she asked, as she wrapped up the last of the presents and forced it into an already full stocking.

'Your guess is as good as mine. He asked if I was Mr Dean, wished me a jolly Christmas, and rang off.'

'One of your fellow drunken workers.'

'I'm a drunken worker?'

'Not very often.' She stood, arching her back. 'I'm getting old.'

'You don't look any different from when I married you.'

'I looked old then?'

They laughed. 'I'll take Leo's stocking and put it in his bedroom,' she said.

'Will that prevent his invading us at five in the morning?'

'Of course not.'

Twenty minutes later they were in bed; three minutes later she prodded him with the heel of her left foot. 'Are you going to read all night?'

He closed the book, put it down, switched off the light.

He had been reading, but his mind had been on the phone call, not the printed words. The caller had not sounded drunk; he was almost certainly not anyone from the office: a friend would surely not have rung so late or spoken so briefly; the laugh had held a quality he found almost impossible to define, yet which had been disturbing ... He remembered the difficulty Kay had had back in October when she had been trying to describe the quality of the laugh of the man who had rung and spoken about white lilies and a coffin.

It was a long time before he fell asleep.

Presents, laid around the base of the Christmas tree, would not be opened until after breakfast had been eaten and the table cleared, no matter how vigorously Leo demanded just a peek.

Dean, on the excuse of wanting to check if he'd left something in the car, went out to the garage and used his mobile to ring Geraldine, Harry and Jane's daughter, who lived in Teddington. He asked her for the phone number of the house in Marbella in which her parents were staying and she gave him it. He dialled the string of numbers and the call was answered after only four rings.

'It's Jerome, Harry. A Merry Christmas to Jane and you.'

'Many thanks and our best to you. And because it's the festive season, I won't tell you there still isn't a cloud in the sky.'

'You know you asked me to get a present for Leo...'

'You're not going to say you forgot? I'll get the blame for that...'

'Kay bought him one of the games that he's been wanting for ages. I'm ringing to know if you're quite certain Jane didn't send, or get someone else to send, Leo a present?'

'She assured me she hadn't, so who am I to doubt?'

'Have a word with her, will you, and see if she could possibly have forgotten she had sent Leo a two-pound box of chocolates shaped like characters from cartoons.'

'Hang on.'

Jane said, 'Merry Christmas, Jerome. About a box of chocolates – I can assure you I didn't send one to Leo. I don't believe in stuffing children with sweets.'

'You are absolutely certain?'

'For goodness sake, you're worse than Harry! He's no memory, but accuses me of never remembering anything; typically male. I repeat, I have not sent a box of chocolates to Leo. Does that satisfy you?'

'Yes. Thanks.'

'What's this all about?'

'He's received a box and we don't know who sent it, so we can't put a name down on the thank-you letter list.'

'I expect you'll find out who it was;

someone will ask if he enjoyed them ... Harry said you bought him a computer game on our behalf?'

Five minutes later he said goodbye and switched off the mobile. He returned to the house.

'Did you find you had?' Kay asked.

'Had what?'

'You said you were going out to see if you'd left something in the car.'

'I hadn't.'

'What did you think you'd left?'

'The keys.'

'Wouldn't it have been easier to check the pegs on which we keep them here, in the kitchen?'

'I didn't think.'

'Obviously.'

He judged she was wondering what had been his real motive for going out? Like so many wives, she had a knack of knowing when he was trying to hide something. He hoped she would not divine what that something was. He crossed to the door into the hall.

'Breakfast will be in five minutes,' she said, as she spooned ground coffee into the coffee machine.

'Are Muriel and Piers up?'

'I've called them, but I haven't heard any movements as yet.'

'Where's Leo?'

'Still upstairs, enjoying the contents of his stocking. Give him a shout to come down and have his breakfast – not that he'll eat much because of excitement.'

He went through the hall and into the sitting room. For one panicky moment, he couldn't remember what colour paper the box of chocolates had been re-wrapped in, then memory returned. From amongst the presents around the Christmas tree, he picked it up.

Because the house was built around the large central fireplaces and chimneys of the sitting and dining rooms, there was a very short, narrow passage on the opposite side to the hall that connected the two rooms. Here, at a height of five feet and recessed in steps that were the obverse of the brickwork of the sitting-room fireplace, was a very small cupboard, which was never used, not only because of its size, but also because of the relative difficulty of access. He was just able to fit the box inside. Kay was very unlikely to look there by chance.

* * *

After Leo had been born and Kay had been told she was unlikely to be able to have another child, she had declared that he might be an only, but he was not going to be spoiled. That her words had not been followed as strictly as she had intended became evident when Leo unwrapped the last of his many parcels and, suffering from satiety, showed little interest in a present that should have pleased him.

'There should be one more,' Kay said.

'There isn't,' Dean said.

'I can see that.' She spoke cryptically, hoping Leo would not understand he was indirectly involved in the conversation. 'Where's the you-know-what?'

'How's that?'

'You know what I mean.'

'I haven't the slightest idea.'

'The what-nots from the unknown that caused so much trouble.'

He could no longer pretend not to understand. 'You wrapped it up.'

'I know that. And I put it with everything else.'

'You can't have done.'

'I most certainly did.'

234

He shrugged his shoulders.

'I can distinctly remember ... Still, it must be around somewhere and maybe it's better if it doesn't appear for a while.' She stood. 'I must make certain the cooking's all right.'

'Can I help,' Muriel asked, 'or is the kitchen off limits?'

'Very much on-limits, if you don't mind doing the Brussels sprouts.'

Dean watched them leave, thankful that Kay had had too many other things to think about to pursue the whereabouts of the missing present.

Kay and Dean returned from the Boxing Day shoot a little after five. Leo met them at the front door, grabbed the pheasants – every gun was given a brace – and, shouting imaginary shots, rushed into the sitting room to show them to the Norrises. Dean carried his leg-of-mutton gun case into the end room – office, library, depository for anything that couldn't find a home anywhere else – and put it on the table, then slid out his gun. He broke it, cleaned and very lightly oiled the barrels, slipped them into the butt, clipped home the fore-end, set it in one of the three unoccupied rests in the

235

cupboard, emptied his cartridge belt and bag, put the cartridges back into boxes on the shelf, closed the metal door and locked it.

When he entered the sitting room (warmed by a good fire), coffee pot, milk jug, sugar bowl, cups, saucers and several mince pies were on a tray on one of the piecrust tables.

'Was it a good day?' Norris asked.

'There were some reasonable birds,' he answered, as he poured himself a cup of coffee, 'but it needed more wind to get them really up.'

'Jerome,' Muriel said, 'will you persuade your son to remove the corpses?'

'Sorry about that ... Leo, take them through to the kitchen, please.' He watched his son leave, incorrectly holding the birds by their legs. Muriel was against blood sports, but not averse to roast pheasant. He added milk and sugar to his coffee, put a mince pie on the saucer, and sat down.

'By the way,' Norris said, 'there was a phone call for you just before lunch. I told him you were out and asked his name, but he said you wouldn't know who he was. Sounded rather odd. Do you know any odd friends?'

'Present company doesn't answer you?'

'Walked into that one, didn't I? Anyway, he hoped you'd had a good Christmas and would enjoy all he wished you.'

'I wonder who on earth that could have been?' Kay said.

'Haven't a clue,' Dean replied.

Eighteen

Dean parked outside Divisional HQ and made his way to the front room. There he explained to a PC that he wanted to speak to DC Tudor; he was asked to wait and did so for twenty minutes, then was shown into a small, soulless interview room. As he put the box of chocolates on the table, at the inner end of which was a recording unit, Tudor hurried in.

'Sorry to keep you, Mr Dean, but today it seems all hell's broken loose. If you'd like to tell me what the problem is ...?' And 'quickly' was unspoken.

'There was a phone call on Christmas Eve from a man who hoped I'd have a jolly Christmas, laughed, and rang off.'

'That worried you?' Tudor tried to hide his impatience.

'I didn't know who he was and his laugh

suggested he hoped I'd have a bloody lousy Christmas.'

'Sounds do get distorted on a telephone line.'

'Not that distorted. He was mocking me. It was the same kind of laugh as so upset my wife. Do you remember her telling you about that?'

'Of course.'

'The laugh made me look down at the identification panel.'

'You made a note of the numbers?'

'I was too late because he rang off seconds after I looked. All I can say is, there were so many numbers it had to be a call from abroad. That made me think of the box of chocolates. It had been posted in Spain and was addressed to our son and the only people likely to send him a present from there, hadn't. You told me the man persecuting us had gone abroad – to Spain?'

'We're not certain,' Tudor lied.

Dean hesitated, then said in a rush of words, 'I know I made a fool of myself suggesting the chocolates were another pipe bomb, but what if there is something wrong with them?'

'Such as?'

'They might be poisoned,' he said defiantly, because he was prepared to meet scornful disbelief.

Tudor said nothing.

'We'd put the box out with all the other presents, so after that phone call, I removed and hid it. On Boxing Day, my wife and I went on a shoot and when we returned home, friends who were staying with us said there'd been a phone call for me from a man who wouldn't give his name, but sent the message he hoped I'd enjoy all he wished me. I'm certain that what he was wishing me was whatever hell he could think up.'

Tudor studied the parcel in front of Dean. 'Those are the chocolates?'

Dean unwrapped the box.

'Do you still have the original wrapping paper?'

'One of the members of the bomb squad tore that off. I can't say what happened to it.'

'If you could try to trace it.' Tudor reached across to slide the box to his side of the table. He lifted the lid by holding it at the corners and used a pencil to push the corrugated white paper to one side. Each chocolate rested in a shaped depression.

'They don't look as if they've been disturbed.'

'You're saying I'm thinking and talking nonsense?'

'Hardly. After all, if someone did set out to lace the chocolates with something, he'd have made certain it wasn't obvious ... I'll arrange to have them examined.'

'I hope ... I hope to God I have been ridiculous and they are nothing more than chocolates.'

And he, Tudor thought, would have reason, when the DI heard about this, to hope they were something more.

On the tenth of January, Naylor paced between desk and window. 'I confess I am at a loss,' he said, after five turns. He came to a halt by his chair. 'At a complete loss to know if I am dealing with a simpleton or an idiot.'

Was there much difference between them? Tudor wondered.

'I thought I had made it crystal-clear we were not going to devote all our resources to nursemaiding the Deans. Obviously, I was mistaken. Mistaken, because I believed I was addressing someone with a modicum of intelligence.' He slapped the palm of his hand down on a sheet of paper on his desk. 'Do you know what that is?'

'No, sir.'

'Internal accounting from the Forensic Science Service laboratory at Itchley. The standard charge for carrying out certain analyses has been debited to the Division's account. Only I don't know a bloody thing about any analyses. Sergeant Unwin is equally ignorant of them, but he did suggest that you might be able to assist us. Can you?'

'Sir, Mr Dean came to the station just over a week ago with a box of chocolates...'

'To show his appreciation of all you have done for him?'

'He was afraid the chocolates had been poisoned.'

'A man of even greater imagination than you?'

'I had reason to think his fear might be justified.'

Naylor stopped pacing, pulled out his chair, and sat. 'I intend to speak to the superintendent and gain his agreement to your transfer to uniform. If asked, I would express the belief that you are likely to find life in uniform no less difficult than it has proved to be in the CID and it must be in your best interests to seek work outside the force. That is all.'

Tudor left. In the CID general room, empty except for himself, he sat and despondently asked himself why he hadn't spoken to Unwin to request the authority to send the chocolates to the laboratory for testing, thereby insulating himself from the consequences? To ask the question was to know the answer. Unwin would have refused the request, leaving Dean ever more frightened, because he wouldn't know whether or not his fears had been justified.

A PC came into the room. 'Busy as usual?'

'Thinking,' Tudor replied briefly.

'CID has learned to do that?' He put an envelope down on Tudor's desk. 'This came along with other papers just delivered ... By the way, do I put you down for two tickets?'

'Tickets for what?'

'CID has learned to think, but not to read? The New Year party, of course. Thirty quid a couple for nosh and almost all the booze you can swallow.'

'OK.'

'You'd better cheer up before then or

you'll likely be wasting your thirty quid.' The PC left.

Tudor stared at the envelope, his thoughts elsewhere. It had become the controversial policy to transfer members of CID back to uniform for a period to prevent (in the words of the Chief Constable) a sense of elitism developing. His transfer would not be part of that scheme; it would be recognized as demotion and a black mark. He had passed his sergeant's exams with flying colours; promotion, Hazel and he had agreed, would be the signal for their marriage. But promotion became much more difficult when one's record was stained with a black mark ... The DI had been unable to decide whether he was a simpleton or a fool. He was both for putting his career at risk for the sake of someone to whom he owed no specific duty.

He opened the envelope, read and reread what was written. Quite suddenly, the sun was shining even though a gentle drizzle had been falling from an overcast sky since daybreak. He hurried along to the DI's room and, since the door was ajar, knocked and entered.

'Yes?' said Naylor aggressively.

'Thought you would want to read this, sir.'

Naylor took the sheet of paper, stared over it at Tudor for several seconds, then lowered his gaze and read. 'I see,' he finally muttered.

Tudor understood he'd been in cloud cuckoo land to expect the DI to apologize.

Dean was checking the papers on his desk, preparatory to returning home, when Julie, nineteen, pert, possessed of little sense of style, entered the room. 'There was a call for you before you returned. Inspector Naylor wants you to ring him as soon as possible – the number's on your desk.'

He looked down at the papers on his desk. 'Where exactly?'

She came forward, pointed. 'I put it there. You've muddled everything up.'

'Then use your feminine skills at finding something a male has lost.'

She began to sort through the papers. He wondered, with curiosity rather than lewd interest, whether she was aware that when she leaned forward, the front of her dress parted until it became obvious she did not wear a brassière and whether she was indifferent to that fact or deliberately

and contemptuously challenged male interest?

She found the piece of paper she sought.
'Do you want me to get the number?'

'I can just about manage to do that.'

She flashed him a smile and left; she had a
neat bottom. He lifted the receiver and
dialled; when the connexion was made, he
asked to speak to Naylor.

'Thanks for ringing,' Naylor said. 'Certain
information has come to hand and you need
to know what that is.'

'Is this to do with the chocolates?'

'I would prefer to speak to you directly.'

'Then I'll come along right away.'

Dean was shown into the interview room
in which he had spoken to Tudor some days
before. Unwilling to sit, nervous, he began
to read the framed list of witness's rights,
detailed in terms that only a dedicated
bureaucrat could have provided. He had
reread the circumstances in which a witness
was entitled to ask for his own legal re-
presentative to be present before being
questioned – and still was not certain he
understood what those were – when Naylor,
followed by Tudor, entered.

Social greetings over, they sat. Naylor

opened the folder he had placed on the table. 'The situation is this, Mr Dean: because in the circumstances you were, naturally, suspicious of the box of chocolates that had been sent to your son, you asked Constable Tudor to have the chocolates examined. They were sent to a forensic laboratory, which conducted analyses, and it is their report that has caused me to contact you.' He picked up a sheet of paper from the folder. 'All the chocolates were tested; about a third were found to contain a foreign substance, which had been injected into them.'

'What was it?'

He read out the name with some difficulty. 'Lysergic acid diethylamide. That is better known as LSD.'

'Christ! ... He intended to murder Leo.'

'My understanding from the report is, it cannot be stated with certainty that death would have resulted from his eating a few of the contaminated chocolates. There is no set toxic dose of LSD because effects vary very considerably from one person to another, which means there is the possibility the intention was to harm your son, rather than to kill him – the normal effects include hallucinations, visual illusions, hyperexcit-ability, convulsions and coma. Of course, considering the age of your son, and the possibility of his eating a great number of chocolates in a short time, death might have been the outcome.'

'The man's mad,' Dean said hoarsely. 'You've got to arrest him now, before he tries anything else.'

'As soon as the presence of LSD was discovered, the box, internal packing and chocolates were subjected to every possible test, regrettably without result ... Were you able to recover the paper in which the box had been wrapped when you received it?'

'My wife thinks it was lying about on the lawn in the morning and she picked it up and put it in the dustbin.'

'Which has been emptied?'

'Days before Mr Tudor asked me about it.'

Naylor began to tap on the table with the fingers of his right hand.

'You know who it is, don't you?'

'We have identified someone who might be able to help us with our inquiries.'

'Don't you ever call a spade a goddamn shovel?'

'A luxury seldom permitted to us.'

'You know who he is and he's in Spain. So for God's sake, arrest him before he succeeds in murdering one or all of us.'

'On the evidence in hand, I'm afraid we could not present a valid case for extradition.'

'And when he comes back to this country? Are you going to go on saying there's nothing you can do?'

'We are bound by the law.'

'But he isn't, so he'll always hold the high ground; but you don't seem to understand that he'll be able to try and try again until he succeeds.'

'I understand how you feel...'

'I am certain you haven't the faintest conception.'

'Mr Dean...' There was a knock on the door and a PC looked into the room. 'What the devil do you want?' Naylor demanded angrily.

'Sorry, sir, but the superintendent says he must have a word with you right away.'

Naylor stood. 'If you'll excuse me ... I'll be back as soon as possible.' He left.

Dean's mind raced. The chocolates had been poisoned. Had he left the box with all the other presents at the foot of the

249

Christmas tree, Leo would inevitably have eaten his fill despite Kay's admonitions, and would have either died or suffered possible permanent mental damage. The police were convinced they knew who the man was, but could not act ... He spoke abruptly. 'His name?'

'How's that?' Tudor's thoughts had been elsewhere.

'What's the name of the man who's trying to murder us?'

'I'm afraid I can't tell you, Mr Dean.'

'On the contrary, you can, but you won't. Like the detective inspector, you're so subservient to the rules, you're prepared to see my son, my wife, or me, perhaps all three of us, murdered rather than help.'

'Giving you a name would change nothing.'

'It would give me the chance.'

'To do what?'

'To tell him to his face he has no reason to want to harm my family or me.'

'He has already been told that several times. I'm sorry, but I don't think anything you could say would have the slightest effect because of the kind of person he is.'

'You think, but you don't know. Even if

you're right, I'd have tried. Can you begin to understand what it's like – not being able to do anything to try to save my family?'

As compassion battled with loyalty to his duty, Tudor wished himself a thousand miles away. He'd been told he had too much imagination. He had. He could imagine all too clearly the fear and desperation in Dean's mind because he knew how he'd suffer if Hazel were threatened and he was not able to help her. 'Mrs Weatherspoon,' he said.

'It's a man who's been trying to murder us, not a woman.'

Naylor returned, remained standing. 'I'm afraid something very urgent has cropped up, Mr Dean, so I'll have to leave you. Constable Tudor will be able to answer any more questions you may have. Please rest assured that we have done, are, and will be, doing everything we possibly can.' He nodded a goodbye, hurried out and shut the door.

'Who's Mrs Weatherspoon?' Dean asked hoarsely.

'An elderly lady who lives in south Redford and is a neighbour of Lynch.'

'Who's Lynch?'

'He was Hopkins's partner.'

'You're telling me...'

'I'm telling you only that it's not often one is asked to look after goldfish very carefully, but Mrs Weatherspoon was when Lynch went to Spain, so it's possible she can give you information that I may not ... Unless you have any more questions, I think there's nothing more to be said.'

'I imagine,' Dean said slowly, 'I owe you my sincere thanks.'

'I've no idea why.'

' "Where ignorance is bliss, 'Tis folly to be wise." '

'Quite likely.'

The young woman in the public library – unknown to Dean, she could have identified Lynch – suggested he consult the council tax lists. The middle-aged man in the council tax office was less than helpful, but eventually agreed to provide the address of Mrs Edith Weatherspoon, who lived in south Redford: number 4 Well Road.

The front door of number 4 was opened to the length of a safety chain; Mrs Weatherspoon regarded him through the gap and demanded to know what he wanted. His

explanation, appearance and manner, persuaded her it was safe to let him enter.

She was elderly, but far from old, and
made him think of a chirpy sparrow as she
showed him into the front room, over-
furnished but so spotlessly clean a speck of
dust must have felt lonely, and suggested he
sat in the far chair, because the nearer one
was not as strong as it should be and
although her nephew had promised to try to
repair it, he never managed to find the time
to do so. The cover of the cushion, she
explained, had been stitched by her before
her eyesight had become poor. He praised
her skill before he moved the cushion and
sat.

'You want to speak to Edgar?' she said.

'I need to tell him something important,
but he's gone off to Spain and I don't know
how to get hold of him; I was hoping you'd
be able to give me an address.'

'But he's not gone to Spain.'

Dean knew the sudden ice of failure as all
the assumptions he'd been making threatened to collapse into chaos.

'He's gone to Majorca.'

Relief was as great as had been despair.

'He and Keith always had a winter holiday

in a rented villa and they kept telling me how they were so looking forward to this one. Keith used to say it gave them fresh energy. Then, poor man, he died. I expect you knew that?'

'Yes, I did.'

'He was such a nice man. Never minded giving me a hand if I needed help. Last year, a shelf broke and he came and fitted a new one. It was terrible to hear what happened.'

'I gather his death really upset Edgar?'

'Of course it did. He became so unhappy, I ... Well, when he used to talk so wildly, saying someone would have to pay for Keith's death, I began to fear he was becoming disturbed in his mind, if you understand what I mean, and might try to kill himself. Thank goodness, he didn't.'

'He's in Majorca now?'

'When I saw how terribly upset he became, I told him he must go on the holiday they'd booked because the change would be such a help for him; at first he said he couldn't possibly go there without Keith, but in the end he did. I do hope he comes back feeling better.'

'I'm sure he will. How long has he gone for?'

'Several weeks, I think. The library agreed to give him extra time off on compassionate grounds.'

'When did he leave?'

'Before Christmas.'

'Whereabouts on the island is he staying?'

'He gave me an address in case I needed to get in touch with him, but I've lost the paper on which I wrote it down – I looked for it only the other day and couldn't find it. It doesn't matter, though, because he rang me last night to ask how the goldfish were and I told him I'd lost it and he gave me a phone number so that I could get in touch with him if I needed to. I think ... Maybe I'm talking very silly, but now that Keith's dead, I think his goldfish give him something to care for and that's why he's so worried he had to ring to find out they're all right.'

'Perhaps you'd give me his telephone number so I can have a word with him?'

She hesitated, then said, 'I don't see why not. Shall I write it down for you – there are rather a lot of numbers?'

'That would be very kind.'

Ten minutes later he settled behind the wheel of his car, certain he knew the truth. Lynch was their tormentor – emotionally shattered by the death of Hopkins, determined to make someone pay for what had happened, now holidaying in Spain. And since he was staying in Majorca for several weeks, there was time for him to try to murder again. While there, the only way in which to pursue the blood feud was by post – so any mail from Spain, or perhaps from a country close to Spain since he might post a deadly letter or parcel from Portugal or France to avoid suspicion, had to be treated as dangerous ... But having so far met failure, mightn't he decide on more direct action? Perhaps he would hire a hit man. What better alibi than to be a thousand miles from the crime? He himself would be the hit man's primary target, but Kay and Leo could so easily become inadvertently involved. Then all the time the three of them were together, he might indirectly be responsible for their suffering. His decision to face Lynch and make him understand he had not shot Hopkins was brutally reinforced.

He waited until after supper before he told Kay about the chocolates.

At first, it seemed she would be able to

accept without too great an emotional reaction the fact that Leo had nearly suffered
mental injury or death; then, quite suddenly, she panicked.

'The police have to arrest him,' she said
violently.

'Unless they find more evidence, they say
they cannot.'

'Then what are we going to do? Just wait
for the bastard to kill Leo or you?'

It took a long time to persuade her it was
necessary for Leo and her to stay with
Muriel and Norris while he flew to Majorca
and made Lynch accept the truth.

Nineteen

When Dean left Gatwick, the grey, lowering clouds had promised rain; when he arrived at Aeroport de Son Sant Joan, the sky was cloudless, the air warm and invigorating. After retrieving his suitcase, he made his way to an information kiosk at which there was an attractive woman who spoke English fluently. He explained he wanted to drive to a friend who was on the island, but stupidly had left the address at home; he had the phone number and had phoned, but there had been no answer and there was no knowing how long his friend would be out. Could she suggest any way in which he might trace the address from the phone number without searching through hundreds of thousands— She stopped him. What was the number? He passed her the slip of paper on which it was written. The fourth and fifth numbers, she explained, showed the address to be in Llorell; the telephone directory was area-sectionalized so all he would have to do was search the numbers listed under Llorell; she had a directory, so if he would like to look...

There were seventeen pages of four-column entries, which suggested it was still going to be something of a task; but he was in luck. Ca'n Tamrin, owned by Beasley, R., was in urbanización Sa Mela, s/n (no road number, she explained). He thanked her and made his way, not without difficulty due to the labyrinthine design, out of the building.

The driver at the head of the line said he spoke English good. He didn't, nor did he drive a taxi good; nevertheless some fifty minutes later and several incidents after leaving the airport, having passed thousands of almond trees beginning to break into a flood of white blossom, they reached the town of Llorell.

Urbanización Sa Mela stretched from level, pine-wooded land up the side of a mountain until the slope became too severe for even a Majorcan to see profit in building on it. Once in the *urbanización*, the driver asked directions from a man who was clearing weeds with a mattock, then continued up to the second lateral road, along which he stopped outside an open gateway. He stared down at the house, some ten metres below, and said he was not driving down that precipice. A wise decision, Dean thought, considering the other's skill behind the wheel; it would have been easy to go *down* the steep slope to the small level area in front of the house and garage, but the return would have called for accurate and controlled driving. Above and beyond the many roof levels of the house was a view to massage an estate agent's hyperbole. Flat land, divided irregularly into small fields bounded by dry-stone walls, on which was an occasional building, stretched to a large bay ringed with mountains.

He walked down the steep slope, thankful for the rope handrail, crossed to the panelled front door and rang the bell. The door was opened by a middle-aged, solidly built woman who wore an apron over a black dress. He asked her if Mr Lynch was in. She replied in broken English that the *señor* was out. The way in which she looked at him caused him to think she was making a false assumption.

Back in the taxi, Dean asked to be taken to a hotel. The driver said it was a no-good time of the year because few tourists and hotels *kaput*, but because he was a smart *hombre*, he would find one open in the port.

Once a small fishing village, in the season Port Llorell had become a thriving holiday centre with a large marina. They drove past a sign banning vehicles, over a curb on to a pedestrian-only way, and along to Hotel Terranova. The driver, showing an enthusiasm not previously evident, carried the suitcase into the foyer and spoke to the receptionist at some length – claiming commission, Dean decided. The conversation concluded, the driver asked for a hundred euros. Dean pointed out that at the airport there had been a list, which specified the fare to Port Llorell as being considerably less than a hundred. The driver, far from showing resentment, touched his arm in a typical gesture and said the *señor* was no damn tourist and therefore the drive would cost only seventy euros, despite searching for the house. He accepted the ten-euro tip with graceful condescension.

It was seven o'clock, yet the air was still

warm enough to sit out on the small bedroom balcony in a cane chair, which creaked with every movement. Beyond the road were the empty beach and the bay, its far shore marked by twin clusters of lights, direct and reflected. He checked the Norrises' phone number – noted on a slip of paper by Kay because he was bound to forget it if left to his memory – and dialled. The connexion was soon made. Piers said he'd call Kay, who was upstairs. Thirty seconds later, she asked, 'Have you seen him?'

'I've found the house where he's staying, but the woman who was doing the cleaning said he wasn't at home. I'll try again tomorrow morning.'

'You've got to keep calm whatever he says or does.'

'I'll be ice cold,' he assured her. 'How are things with you?'

'Fine.'

'All's smooth with Muriel and Piers?'

'They're being wonderful. She gets on so well with Leo and at lunch time Piers said we were to stay just as long as we wanted to.'

'With any luck, I'll soon be back home.'

'You really think...' She stopped.

'He'll have to believe me.'

'I hope to God you're right.'

'I usually am.'

'A big-headed optimist.'

'Surely preferable to a small-minded pessimist?'

'I'll take you whichever, my love.'

After the call was over, he returned to the chair on the balcony. He hoped his confidence had sounded genuine.

The taxi driver who took him from the port to the *urbanización* spoke English with inaccurate fluency – a fact that had its disadvantage, since he was keen to point out Manchester United's inferiority to Real Madrid.

They came to a stop in front of the driveway down to Ca'n Tamrin. The driver studied it for a moment. 'You walk.'

It seemed Majorcan drivers lacked a certain confidence. 'I shouldn't be very long.'

'I no wait for ever.'

Dean made his way down the curving slope, holding tightly on to the rope handrail. The front door was opened by a man, several years younger than he, dressed in what passed for smart fashion in the world of modern youth. He had tight curly black hair, softly handsome features, and a petulant expression.

'Is Mr Lynch here?' Dean asked.

The man stared at him for a while, then said angrily, in broad estuary English, 'He ain't.' He slammed the door shut.

Dean phoned soon after ten on Tuesday morning.

'Yes?'

The voice identified the speaker as the man he had faced at Ca'n Tamrin the previous evening. 'Is Mr Lynch in?'

'Who wants to know?'

'My name's John Metcalfe – not that it will mean anything to Mr Lynch. I'm a friend of Mrs Weatherspoon.'

'Hang on.'

There was a short wait and then another man said, 'Was it you called here yesterday?'

'That's right.'

'Do I know you?'

'We haven't met, but as I explained...'

'What d'you want?'

'Edith learned I was coming out to this island and asked me to get in touch to tell you everything at Well Road is fine and the

264

goldfish are flourishing.'

The mention of the goldfish seemed to reassure Lynch and he spoke with slight friendliness. 'Good of you to let me know. Most kind.'

It seemed the thanks were intended as a cut-off. 'She also gave me something to give to you.'

'What's that?'

'I've no idea as it's well wrapped up. I've been along twice so I'd like to make certain it's third time lucky.' He chuckled. 'When's the best time to bring it along?'

After a pause, Lynch said, 'I'll be here at twelve tomorrow.'

Dean said he looked forward to the meeting and rang off. He found he was sweating.

As Dean made his way down the steep drive, he reminded himself he must keep calm. But, came the question, how did he keep calm when facing the man who had tried to kill him and his family?

He went around a Seat Ibiza taking up much of the flat area in front of the house, and rang the bell. The door was opened by a man noticeably shorter than he, slightly built, with lank, untidy hair. 'Mr Lynch?'

'That's me.'

He shook hands. Lynch's grip was flabby. Appropriate, Dean thought, considering the very pale-blue, close-set eyes and weak, crooked mouth. For a moment, he wondered if this really could be the man who had sent the letter, made the phone call, thrown the brick, posted the pipe bomb, injected the chocolates; but then hatred was often a sign of character weakness.

He stepped into the hall. As he did so, a door to the right opened and the man to whom he had spoken on his previous visit appeared, came to a stop, stared at him and said, 'What's happening?'

'It's not like that, Georgy,' Lynch said hurriedly.

'You could bleeding fool me for a start.'

'He's a friend of a neighbour at home who's brought me a present.'

'Enjoy it before I stuff it up—'

'You've got it all wrong.'

'You think I'm soft? Can't see what's parked in front of me?'

'Georgy, I swear—'

'You make me want to puke!' He pulled open the front door, went out and slammed it shut behind him.

Lynch hurriedly opened the door and called out. By way of an answer, Georgy started the engine of the Ibiza and revved it fiercely, drove recklessly quickly up to the road.

'I told him yesterday ... Why did you have to come here?' Lynch demanded shrilly. 'Why did the stupid bitch tell you where I was?' He crossed to the door on his left, hurried into the kitchen. Bottles clinked, a glass was dropped and smashed; he swore violently.

Dean went into the sitting room and over to the French windows, stepped out on to the balcony, and tried to gain a sense of calm from the beauty in front of him.

When Lynch finally came into the sitting room, it was clear that the half-filled glass in his hand had already been emptied at least once. 'Why d'you have to come here with him already being so aggro because of Tony?' he demanded. 'He wouldn't listen when I told him Tony...' He drank. 'Why did the old bitch give you something; why didn't she wait for me to get back?'

Dean said, 'My name is not Metcalfe. It is Jerome Dean.'

Lynch had begun to walk, a shade unsteadily, to one of the chairs; he stopped, turned so sharply he lost his balance and had hurriedly to reach with his free hand for support. Liquid slopped out of his glass.

'I've come here because it's the only way to stop you trying to kill me and my family.'

'You're the bastard who murdered my Keith,' he shouted.

'No one murdered him. He was shot accidentally by a Frenchman who could not know your friend was hiding in the wood.'

'You bleeding liar.'

'It is the truth. The Frenchman was next to me when he fired and your friend was hit.'

'It's you who murdered him.'

'Would I be here if I had?'

Lynch drained his glass.

'The police carried out a full investigation into the shooting and came to the firm conclusion that I did not fire the fatal shot. The detectives told you that.'

'They were lying, all of 'em.'

'If they'd believed I'd fired that shot, if they'd even thought that possible, do you really think they would have lied to you to save me?'

Lynch left the room. When he returned, his glass was full.

268

'Since you weren't at the shoot, what makes you believe it was me who killed your friend?'

He drank.

'Tell me and I'll prove why you're wrong.'

'I know it was you,' he shouted.

'Then you know nothing. You've been frightening my wife...'

'You murdering sod!' He drained the glass and threw it to the floor, sending slivers across the tiles. 'If she'd burned to death, I'd have laughed, knowing you were suffering like I was.'

'You're mad,' Dean said thickly. His belief that Lynch would listen to reason had been mere wishful thinking; all this meeting had achieved was to increase the other's hatred.

He left.

Twenty

The taxi stopped in front of the main entrance of Palma airport and Dean climbed out; the driver opened the boot of the Mercedes, lifted out the suitcase and put it down on the pavement, closed the boot, accepted the fare and generous tip with grunted thanks, returned to his seat behind the wheel and drove off.

Dean stared at the fountains, their jets sparkling in the sunshine, the walkways – yet again not walking – and the crowd of newly arrived tourists, mostly elderly, making for two of the parked buses, no doubt looking forward to pleasure. He was retreating from failure.

He entered the building and followed the signs to the check-in area, where overhead screens directed him to desk number 23. He joined a queue. Immediately ahead of him, two teenage girls discussed the past week in

270

intimately implausible terms, careless that they could be overheard. The queue moved forward slowly. The two girls checked in their cases and giggled when the woman behind the desk hoped they had had a good stay as she handed back their tickets. He put his suitcase on the conveyor, passed her his ticket; she indicated a notice, in English, French, German and Spanish, calling for passports to be shown. He handed her his.

'Please wait,' she said in English. She placed his ticket and passport on the working surface by her side.

'Is something wrong?'

She lifted his suitcase off the conveyor and put it by the side of her seat. She flashed a smile. 'You please wait.' She looked past him. 'Next.'

'Would you tell me...' he began.

'*Señor*,' said a man who, unnoticed by him, had walked up to stand by his side.

'What?'

The man spoke in Spanish.

'I'm afraid I don't understand.'

'You are to go with him,' she said, her fingers poised above the keyboard of the computer terminal.

'Why?'

'I cannot tell.'

'Doesn't he understand I have a plane to catch...'

'*Señor*,' said the man a second time as he firmly gripped Dean's arm.

'What the devil's going on?'

'You are Señor Dean?' asked a second man, in understandable English.

'Yes.'

'Please to come with us.' He spoke to the woman behind the counter. She handed him Dean's ticket and passport, indicated the suitcase and, with obvious resentment when he did not move forward, lifted it up and put it on the motionless conveyor.

'Call the police,' Dean said loudly.

'They are police,' she replied.

'What do they want?'

'Your passport, your ticket, your suitcase. And you,' she added as an afterthought.

One of the men picked up the suitcase, then they escorted him out of the building and along to a car parked near the taxi rank. They asked him to sit in the back and when he didn't immediately comply, bundled him in. As he settled on the far side, he decided he'd walked through the mirror into Kafka land.

The room was small and bleak, its only furnishing a table, four chairs, and an empty cupboard. Through the window was a view of Llorell Bay, seen between the trunks of pine trees. Taking advantage of the light but steady wind, several people in wetsuits were windsurfing. The man who sat opposite Dean could have been a mute: every question put to him was met with a shake of the head or a shrug of the shoulders.

The door opened and a small, dapper man, a folder in one hand, entered. He sat. 'Thank you, Señor Dean for agreeing to have a word with us,' he said in good English.

'I don't remember any agreement on my part.'

He smiled briefly, stroking his toothbrush moustache with a forefinger. 'May I introduce myself? I am Inspector Garcia, Cuerpo General de Policia.' He put the folder down on the table. 'I believe that, in your country, that would be called the Criminal Investigation Department.'

'Then you can tell me why I've been dragged here when I should be on a plane flying back to England?'

'You do not understand?'

'No.'

Garcia spoke to the second man, who stood and left. He opened the folder and on top of the few papers were a ticket and passport. 'These are yours. I show them to you so you can be certain they are safe.'

'May I have them?'

'For the moment, no.'

'Why not?'

'Because it may be necessary to speak with you more than this one time and I should wish to be certain that that will be possible.'

'Speak to me about what, for God's sake?' he demanded.

'You would not like to guess?'

'Haven't I made it goddamn clear that I haven't the slightest idea what's going on?'

Garcia tapped on the table with the fingers of his right hand; they were short, stubby fingers and the nails were manicured. His hair was carefully waved, his moustache smoothly trimmed; his suit fitted him with bespoke certainty. He could have been mistaken for a popinjay were one to miss the sharp character beneath the smooth appearance. 'You have been staying at the Hotel Terranova since Monday?'

'Yes.'

'Did you visit, more than once, a house called Ca'n Tamrin which is in the urbanización Sa Mela, between Llorell and Port Llorell?'

'What's the next question? Did I have doughnuts for breakfast?'

'I think you are perhaps referring to *ensaimadas*. You will make things easier, *señor*, if you try to help me.'

'It would make things a damn sight easier for me if I knew what this is all about.'

Garcia continued to speak quietly and pleasantly. 'Did you visit Ca'n Tamrin twice on Monday and once on Wednesday?'

'Yes.'

'For what reason?'

'To speak to Lynch, who is there on holiday.'

'Who *was* staying there.'

'He's left; he's returned to England?' Dean's thoughts raced. Had Lynch, on discovering he was on the island and unable to defend Kay and Leo...

'He has not gone anywhere, Señor Dean. This morning, Mariá-Ferrer, who is employed to clean villas which are rented to foreigners, arrived at Ca'n Tamrin at about

275

nine thirty. Because there seemed to be no one there, she let herself in. She found Señor Lynch had died.'

'Good God!' He stared unseeingly at the far wall. Lynch had not flown home to attack Kay and Leo; he would never again attack anyone. Any other man's death might have diminished him, but not this one. 'What was it – a heart attack?'

'A knife.'

'He had an accident?'

'The preliminary investigation makes accident or suicide very unlikely, but one will have to read the full post-mortem report before one can be certain.'

'Are you saying he was murdered?'

'I think that is so.'

'Then ... Christ! you don't think I had anything to do with that?' It was a stupid question; it was suddenly very clear why he had been brought back from the airport.

'I have to consider every possibility,' Garcia said with unfailing courtesy.

'But this is crazy. Can't you understand...'

'*Señor*, it will save time if I ask the questions and you answer them. I think you visited Ca'n Tamrin three times in all?'

'Yes.'

'And you spoke to Señor Lynch on each occasion?'

'Not the first – twice. I was told he wasn't there even though, the second time, he probably was.'

'Why should you think that?'

'A man told me he was out. I gained the impression he was lying.'

'Was he an Englishman?'

'Yes.'

'Was he a friend of Señor Lynch?'

'I've no idea other than that appearances suggested he was probably a close friend.'

'Mariá Ferrer has spoken about him. She does not know his name or where he lives when he is not staying at Ca'n Tamrin. Can you help me?'

'Lynch called him Georgy, but beyond that I can't tell you anything about him. Look, I swear I didn't even know Lynch was dead...'

'Please, a little time to understand. You do not seem disturbed to learn Señor Lynch is dead, so perhaps he was not a great friend?'

'I'd never met him before yesterday.'

'Then what was your reason for wishing to meet him?'

In the circumstances, with suspicion

brushing him, it was obvious the truth – that he had reason to hate Lynch – must appear incriminating. A good lie could always enjoy two lives. 'I'd been asked by a neighbour of his in England to give him something.'

'What was this?'

'I've no idea. It was small and well wrapped up.'

'When did you visit Señor Lynch yesterday morning?'

'I can't give a definite time.'

'If I suggest you were there at eleven thirty, you will not disagree?'

'Why suggest that time?'

'Because Señor Lynch was heard to have an angry argument with another Englishman who was not his companion you call Georgy at about that time by the French family who are renting the next villa. Sound carries well when the air is still.'

'I had an argument with him, but I wouldn't describe it as angry.'

'What was the argument about?'

'I can't remember.'

'It is unusual to meet a man for the first time and have an argument with him.'

'That depends on what one talks about.'

'So what did you discuss?'

'I've just said, I can't remember.'

'You have a poor memory?'

'For unimportant matters.'

Garcia thought for a moment before he said, 'You have not asked me when it is probable Señor Lynch died.'

'Why should I be interested?'

'I understand. Only the guilty man – if indeed there is a guilty man – would wish to know if he was seen or heard at Ca'n Tamrin at the time Señor Lynch died ... You still cannot remember what your argument with the *señor* was about?'

'No.'

'Perhaps it is of no consequence. Thank you for your help.'

'I'm free to go?'

'Indeed.'

'Then may I have my passport and ticket, which I'll try to get changed?'

'I am sorry, that is not possible yet. There may be more questions to ask you.'

'You're saying I have to stay on the island?'

'If you would be kind enough.'

'A polite way of saying I'm under arrest?'

'You have an expression ... I forget. I fear I do not speak English well.'

'Too well for my choice.'

Garcia smiled. 'I have always admired the English sense of humour. And I have remembered the words: house arrest. Perhaps we might call this, hotel arrest.'

Dean wondered if that was Spanish humour.

He had been unable to ring Kay to tell her he had not caught the plane (she had a mobile, but seldom remembered to have it switched on), but since she was back at home and had not been meeting him by car because of the traffic on the M25, he had time to speak to her before he was due back and could still the fears that otherwise would flood her mind when he failed to arrive.

The hotel had provided him with the room he had vacated that morning – the staff's surprise at his return had been equalled by their curiosity. He sat on one of the twin beds, lifted the receiver and dialled. After four rings, Kay answered.

He told her Lynch had died suddenly and therefore they need no longer fear a further attempt to injure or murder them. She sounded as if she was crying with relief.

'I don't quite know when I'll be returning...' he began.

'Why not?'

'The police have asked me to stay.'

'Why?'

'I think they reckon I may be able to help them.'

'Help them how?'

'I'm damned if I can understand, but it seemed best to go along with what they wanted.'

'But...'

'How are the snowdrops; is there any sign of them yet?' Because of her childhood, snowdrops held a sentimental attraction and a great number were planted around the apple trees.

Twenty-One

The calms of January, with their blue skies and warm sunshine, had abruptly given way to overcast gloom and a north-east wind, which was forecast to bring snow to the mountains. Souvenir shops, most hotels, and some restaurants and bars had now closed, beaches were deserted, no yacht or windsurfer crossed the bay, the waters of which were a sullen green.

Dean's enforced stay became ever more frustrating, since there was nothing to do but explore the island in a hire car – relatively quickly done when so much was shut – walk, read, or watch gormless programmes on English commercial television; and whatever he was doing, his mind struggled with the question: did the police have sufficient nous to understand he knew nothing about Lynch's death? On Saturday morning, he learned the answer to that question.

He returned from a walk along the front and asked for the key of his room. The receptionist said, 'The Cuerpo was here not long before, *señor.*'

'Really.'

The receptionist was far too curious to accept Dean's curt attempt to close the conversation. 'The inspector was wishing to speak to you.'

'May I have my key, please.'

'Since you were not here, he spoke with several members of the staff. He wished to know if we had seen you leave the hotel or return on Wednesday evening. And also, he asked if a guest could leave the hotel without walking through here. Of course, we had to tell him about the staff door, which is at the back of the hotel...'

'I don't give a damn if the inspector was asking how often I brush my teeth. The key.'

The receptionist turned, lifted the key off the board, and handed it to him. 'People say the inspector can be a very mean man.' He spoke with the pleasure of someone who enjoyed other people's misfortunes.

★ ★ ★

Dean was in the small lounge, seated at a marble-topped table and having a pre-lunch drink, when Garcia entered and came across.

'Good morning, *señor*.'

Ingrained manners caused Dean to stand, shake hands, and ask the other if he would like a drink.

'If I might have a *coñac*, *señor*, I should be pleased.'

They sat. The waiter came across and took the order. Garcia produced a pack of cigarettes and offered it.

'I don't. Thanks.'

'You are fortunate.'

An eavesdropper might, Dean thought, absurdly have assumed this to be a social occasion.

'*Señor*, I am here to ask you to come to the Guardia Civil post when you find that it is convenient to you.'

'And if it never is?'

'I do not think you wish for an answer.'

'What do you want now?'

'We have a saying: "When the bottle is empty, there is always a drop left inside." '

'I am not a bottle.'

The inspector smiled.

The waiter returned, put down a glass in front of each of them and a small, earthenware dish filled with black olives between them, picked up the empty glasses and left.

'Health,' Garcia said, as he raised his glass.

Life might have been fractionally more acceptable if the other hadn't been so bloody polite, Dean thought bitterly.

That evening he walked along the front to the large, featureless building, with living quarters at the rear, set back from the coast road. A *cabo* looked up from the magazine he was reading and in tones of annoyance asked him something in Spanish.

He said, 'Inspector Garcia.'

The *cabo* spoke again and when Dean replied that he was sorry, he did not understand Spanish, slammed the magazine down on the desk and left the small room. On his return, Garcia was with him.

'Good evening, *señor*,' Garcia said. 'It is kind of you to come so soon.'

'I gathered that if I didn't, I would be dragged here in chains.'

'It is a long time since we have behaved as energetically as that.' He smiled. 'Now, please, come with me.'

They settled in the same room in which Dean had previously been questioned. Garcia offered him a cigarette, which he refused.

'Of course. I had forgotten.'

By design, no doubt. 'What d'you want?'

Garcia lit a cigarette, dropped the match into an ashtray. 'I should like to ask you a few more questions about certain matters. You should understand that the medical evidence says Señor Lynch could not have killed himself, while the possibility of accidental death is nothing. So we have to know he was murdered. And who murdered him. Death was between twenty-three hundred hours on Wednesday and perhaps nought four hundred hours on Thursday. Naturally, an estimate of time of death is not accurate, but it is all one has. So I should like you to tell me where you were that evening and night?'

'I did not kill him.'

'I still wish to know where you were?'

'It must have been Georgy who killed him. From the very little I saw of Georgy, I'd say the relationship was jagged because of jealousy. That night there must have been a row which, because they'd been drinking heavily, turned very nasty. It'll do you a lot more good to find Georgy and question him rather than me.'

'We have, of course, been trying to identify him. But it is difficult, since there are many English on the island even in winter and we cannot know where he might be because we know nothing about him. Indeed, if he killed Señor Lynch, then one can imagine he will have left the island by now.'

'So lacking him as a suspect, I'll do?'

'I do not quite understand.'

'You need a suspect. If the prime one disappears, choose another.'

'You will not be considered a suspect, *señor*, unless there is very good reason to believe you should be. For now, you are just helping us.' Garcia spoke with quiet resentment when he added: 'We respect the law as much as do the policemen in your country.'

'The English police's respect for the law is blind and comes at a cost to the innocent.'

'Why do you say that?'

Dean silently swore. Reveal his reason for having sought out Lynch and his motive for murder would be established. 'One reads about cases where it seems justice has been of less importance than the rules.'

'I understand. As one of our great writers once said, "God dispenses justice; man can only try to do so." So that is why I ask you to help and tell me where you were on Wednesday night.'

'In the hotel.'

'What were you doing?'

'I had dinner, watched the television until I was totally bored, then went to bed.'

'You did not leave the hotel?'

'As you will have confirmed, having questioned the staff.'

'I am afraid I cannot be as certain as I would wish. One cannot blame the man at the reception desk for not knowing without doubt who he saw leave or return to the hotel days before. But I understand that should a guest wish to leave the hotel without being seen by the receptionist, there is a door for the staff at the back of the hotel.'

'How am I supposed to have known that?'

'It is difficult to say. Perhaps you were careful to search for another way to leave.'

'I did not go out; I was in the hotel all evening and all night.'

Garcia stubbed out the cigarette. 'I wish to know about the argument you had with Señor Lynch.'

'I've told you. I've forgotten what we were arguing about.'

'I can be certain you are an intelligent man; an intelligent man does not easily forget what he was arguing about with a stranger.'

There was a silence.

'Perhaps,' Garcia said slowly, 'you were very disappointed to find Señor Lynch was entertaining the man you say you know only as Georgy?'

'Are you suggesting ... I'm happily married.'

'The situation I am thinking about is not unknown.'

'You can forget it.'

'Very well. Then I must learn what it was you were arguing about?'

'For the umpteenth time, I've forgotten.'

'I do not think so.'

'That's the truth.'

'I will say what I think is the truth. You do not wish to tell me because this argument will provide reason for you to murder Señor Lynch.'

'It's nothing to do with his death.'

'If you cannot remember what it was about, how can you be certain of that?'

'Because I didn't kill the bastard,' Dean said harshly.

'You call him a bastard because clearly you did not like him. Which gives me another question: how can you dislike someone you have only just met?'

'Haven't you ever disliked someone on sight?'

'Perhaps. But I think I have always withheld the description "bastard" until I am certain it is deserved.' Garcia lit another cigarette. 'Thank you for coming here, *señor*. Would you like me to ask someone to drive you to the hotel?'

'I'll walk.' Dean stood. 'When do I get my passport and ticket back?'

'As soon as I am certain you can tell me nothing about Señor Lynch's death.'

'I have said so, time and again.'

'It is I who have to be certain.'

'And I stay here until you are?'

'I fear so.'

'Then as things have been going so far, I'm here for a hell of a long time.'

'It is a beautiful island, even in poor weather.'

Unwin walked into the CID general room

on Tuesday evening. 'Where the hell's every-one?'

Tudor looked up from the computer. 'Out, sarge.'

'Not being blind, I can see that. Out where?'

'Jigger's on the Salington robbery, Rolf's on a course, Ted's sick...'

'Sick of work. Then it'll have to be you. Prepare a report...'

'Please, sarge, not now. I'm taking Hazel out...'

'When the report's finished.'

'She'll go spare if I'm very late again.'

'She went spare the day she agreed to have anything to do with you.'

It wasn't going to be long before she might agree. 'A report on what?'

'The guv'nor's had a request through the usual channels from Spain. They want any information we can provide on Jerome Dean, with particular reference to any known connexion between him and Edgar Lynch.'

'Good God! What's happened?'

'Lynch was found dead with a knife stuck in his guts.'

'Well, I'll be...'

'Never mind what you'll be; get on and draw up all the info we can give.'

'I wouldn't have thought Mr Dean would end up doing something like that. Never can tell. But you can't blame him, can you?'

'If you can't, you've no right to be working this job. And if you can ever learn to understand that, you'll make a better copper than you do now. Another thing to chew on. If you hadn't told Mr Dean where Lynch was having a holiday...'

'I didn't.'

'If you hadn't told him, because you seem to think you're a lovey agony aunt, he wouldn't be out there now, staring at a life sentence in a Spanish jail.' Unwin left.

Tudor tried to mock the detective sergeant's words, but had to accept them. If he had not given Dean the information, this murder would not have happened. Yet he could not feel guilty, as Unwin intended. With Lynch dead, there could be no further danger to Dean and his family. Wasn't a man entitled to defend himself, his wife and his children, as fiercely as a threat demanded – more certainly when he'd been betrayed by the law supposed to defend him?

He went to resume work, but the VDU

was blank. Because of surprise at hearing about the death of Lynch, he must have inadvertently pressed one of the keys and instructed the bloody machine to wipe everything.

'Thank you for coming here,' Garcia said.

'As the spider said to the fly,' Dean remarked sourly.

'Should I suggest I am a vegetarian?'

Was he meant to laugh?

'Do please sit.'

He sat.

'Would you like some coffee?'

The condemned man was, according to tradition, always allowed a last meal of his choice. In winter, ask for fresh strawberries. He said he would like some coffee.

'I will not be long.' Garcia left the room.

Did authority make certain suspects were questioned in rooms that killed all hope? Dean wondered. The patchy brown paint, the stained tiles, the cheap, battered furniture, the barred window could evoke only despair.

Garcia returned. He sat, after hitching up his carefully creased trousers; his white shirt collar might have been starched; his tie was knotted with the precision of a ready-made one, though clearly he was not a man who would indulge in such sartorial slovenliness. 'The coffee will soon be here and I have asked for two croissants. I trust you like them?'

'Yes.'

'I hoped there would still be some *ensaimadas*, but they had all vanished. I believe you have been enjoying them at the hotel? As I expect you know, they are only made on this island. Some say one can also buy them in Barcelona, but I do not know that for fact. For a small island, Majorca produces several delicacies which are nowhere else—'

'Why have you asked me to come here this morning?'

There was a knock on the door and it was opened by a *cabo*, who placed a tray on the table and left.

Garcia passed a plate, offered a larger plate on which were two croissants, suggested Dean help himself to butter and jam, if he liked both, and to sugar and milk for his coffee. 'I have been in England twice and I have to confess that there are many wonderful things to see there, but soon I long to return to Spain and enjoy some coffee. But that is being impolite. In my experience, every country prepares a food or drink better than another – if that were not so, where would be the pleasure to travel? Where in Spain does one eat roast beef as in England? And surely you can suggest many other things that are better in your country than here.'

'I'm sorry, but I don't give a damn what country does what. All that interests me is: why have you dragged me back here? What's happening? My wife is becoming more and more worried by my not returning.'

'*Señor*, everything will be explained.' Garcia tore off a piece of croissant, dunked it in his coffee and ate. 'I was interested in the argument you had with Lynch, a man you had only just met, so I asked England for any information that might help me understand what this was about. Their answer has arrived. You will know what it tells me, of course?'

'No,' Dean answered hoarsely.

'In October of last year, you were invited to a shoot at a big estate. During the morning, a man who wanted to interrupt the shoot because he believed himself to be in sympathy with animals, was accidentally shot and killed. The police investigation confirmed you had not fired the shot, but the dead man's partner, Lynch, believed you had. Lynch wrote you a threatening letter, made a threatening phone call, sent a pipe bomb, which failed to explode but did cause a fire, and finally posted poisoned chocolates to your son, hoping to harm or murder him. The police identified the guilty man, but failed to uncover sufficient evidence to be able to arrest him. Knowing he remained free to pursue you and your family, you learned where he was living. What did you decide to do then?'

Accepting it was ridiculous to deny the facts, Dean said, 'Make him understand I did not fire the fatal shot so that he stopped his insane persecution.'

'Did you succeed?'

'He wouldn't listen to me.'

'Is that what the argument was about?'

'Yes.'

'You learned he hated you so much, he would never believe you and would continue to try to injure your family and you?'

'Yes.'

'Which left you only one way to stop him.'

'I did not kill him.'

'You were convinced he must eventually succeed in injuring or killing someone in your family, yet did nothing?' Garcia stubbed out the cigarette. 'A man's most precious possession is his family; it is his present and future. In ancient days, if it was necessary, a man would kill to protect his family and he was held to be justified; we believe ourselves to be more civilized, so we are required to leave the law to protect innocence, decide guilt, and punish the guilty. But there are rules as to how the law may act and a victim may have to learn that it cannot help him because the rules forbid what is necessary if he is to be helped. In such a case, who will deny him his right to act to save his family and himself? The law will. It is at such a moment that a man will decide he has no option but to kill.'

'I did not murder Lynch,' Dean said, with the desperation of failure.

Garcia lit another cigarette. 'Ask me whether that man is justified when he kills and I must answer that he is not, because I am here to uphold the law. But because I serve it, I am inescapably bound by its rules and therefore, before I arrest someone, I must have proof he is guilty; certainty without proof can never be enough. I do not have the necessary proof that you killed Lynch and am now convinced I never will.'

'What ... what are you saying?'

'I was born in Jerez, *señor*. We Andalucians understand that one's family are more important than any laws.' He produced Dean's passport and ticket and passed them across the table.

Dean sat on the right-hand bed in the hotel bedroom and, like a child unwilling to release his hold on a new present, kept the passport on his lap as he phoned home.

'Yes?'

'My darling, I've just...'

'What's going on?' Kay demanded wildly. 'I'm crazy with worry. I know something is terribly wrong, but you keep trying to make out it isn't.'

'I'm booked on a flight that takes off at seven tomorrow morning and I'll be back with you by midday. Put a bottle of Clicquot in the fridge and we'll crack it the moment I get back.'

There was a long pause. Then she cried 'Jerome! Jerome!', as if in prayer.

Twenty-Two

They sat on opposite sides of one of the window tables in 'Chez Chateaubriand'; behind and above Rourke hung a large, framed aerial photograph of the Kyrenia mountain range. The wine waiter, his Zapata moustache in need of trimming, emptied the bottle of Nuits-Saint-Georges into their glasses.

Sewell raised his glass and savoured the bouquet. 'A pleasant little wine.'

'So it should be at the price,' Rourke observed.

'As Eastleigh said, "Quality is always expensive." '

' "Quality is never expensive," is actually what he wrote.'

'You are a positive mine of erudition,' Sewell observed tartly.

The head waiter came up to their table

and expressed his hope that the gentlemen were enjoying an excellent meal. Sewell said the beef had not been quite as tender as usual. The head waiter offered his regrets in tones that expressed his contempt for a client's opinion. He walked away.

'Don't you think the beef was a little tougher than one normally enjoys here?' Sewell asked.

'I can't really give an opinion, as I haven't eaten here since the last time with you,' Rourke answered. 'Have to keep a firm eye on expenses.'

'Since you're now departmental head, isn't that taking things rather too seriously?'

'Finding my feet, I suppose. By the way, I've been wanting to ask you: was there any fall-out from the ... the little arrangement we discussed back in October?'

'My dear Clive, how you do worry! Naturally there were no unwelcome consequences.' He drank, replaced the glass on the table. 'Although, as a matter of fact ... This is strictly between the two of us.'

'Of course.'

'I suppose one person was affected adversely by the "little arrangement", as you so delightfully call it: Baron Vaillant.'

'If he's discovered something, the authorities are bound to find out...'

'The authorities never learn more than we allow them to. You'll remember my telling you the baron came to England to decide whether it would be more advantageous for the French company Pensec to amalgamate with Sparkson and Tennant or with a German firm, his decision bound to be accepted by the French government. We happened to learn that in truth he had made his decision before arriving on our shores and he favoured the German company – his visit to England was simply a blind, to make it appear there had been honest competition. Perfidious Marianne!'

'I thought I'd read the amalgamation was to go ahead with the English company?'

'Indeed.'

'Then Vaillant suddenly changed his mind?'

'The moment we learned about his underhand manoeuvre, so typical of the Continentals, it became obvious there was now nothing to be lost by advising him that if the investigation into the death of that stupid man was ever pursued, it was likely it would be determined it was he, Vaillant, who had

fired the fatal shot; and that in circumstances which might well involve him on a
charge of manslaughter through criminal
negligence.' Sewell drained his glass. 'The
French have always been a pragmatic people
– selfishly pragmatic, that is to say.'